W9-CNC-086

THE ROAD
TO CAMLANN

By the same author

Beowulf
The Hound of Ulster
The High Deeds of Finn MacCool
Tristan and Iseult
Heather, Oak, and Olive. Three Stories
Blood Feud
Sun Horse, Moon Horse
The Light Beyond the Forest
Frontier Wolf
The Sword and the Circle

THE ROAD
TO CAMLANN

Rosemary Sutcliff

Decorations by
SHIRLEY FELTS

E. P. Dutton   New York

First published in the United States 1982 by
E. P. Dutton, Inc., 2 Park Avenue, New York, N.Y. 10016

Library of Congress Cataloging in Publication Data

Sutcliff, Rosemary.   The road to Camlann.

Summary: The evil Mordred, plotting against his father
King Arthur, implicates the Queen and Sir Lancelot
in treachery and brings about the downfall of Camelot
and the Round Table.
     1. Arthurian romances.   [1. Arthur, King.
        2. Knights and knighthood—Fiction.
           3. Folklore—England] I. Title.
PZ8.1.S95Ro 1982   398.2′2′0942   82-9481
ISBN 0-525-44018-6   AACR2

Printed in the U.S.A.   First Edition
        10 9 8 7 6 5 4 3 2 1

CONTENTS

THE DARKNESS
BEYOND THE DOOR

When the darkness crowds beyond the door, and the logs on the hearth burn clear red and fall in upon themselves, making caverns and ships and swords and dragons and strange faces in the heart of the fire, that is the time for story telling.

Come closer then, and listen.

The story of King Arthur is a long, long story, woven of many strands and many colours; and it falls naturally into three parts.

The first part tells how the father of Arthur, Utha Pendragon, with the help of the enchanter Merlin, won the fair Igraine to be his queen. And when their son Arthur was born, Merlin, knowing by his magic arts that Utha would die before he could count one grey hair in his beard, and that in the struggle for power among the nobles after his death his son would be trampled underfoot, took the babe on the very night he was born, and carried him away and gave him to a certain quiet knight called Sir Ector, to be brought up along with his own son Kay until the time came for him to claim his destiny. But he did not tell even Sir Ector who his fosterling was.

And as Merlin had foreseen, Utha died when his son was but two years old, and the chiefs and nobles of the realm fell to struggling together for power; and the invading Saxons, whom Utha had driven out of Britain, seeing their chance, came storming in again.

And Merlin sorrowfully watched all this and waited, while in his foster-father's castle Arthur grew from a child into a boy and from a boy into a young man. And when Arthur was turned fifteen, Merlin went to the Archbishop Dubricius in London, and told him certain things; and so the Archbishop called a great joust, and all the knights and nobles of the realm came flocking to take part. And when they were gathered, suddenly there appeared in their midst, in the garth of the great abbey, a stone with an anvil set upon it, and driven into the anvil and through it into the stone was a splendid sword. And about the stone was written in letters of gold:

"*Who so pulleth out this sword from this stone*

and anvil is the true-born King of all Britain."

And when the knights and nobles had tried and failed to pull out the sword, Arthur, who was not yet even a knight, but had come to London as a squire to his foster-brother Sir Kay, drew out the sword as easily as from a well-oiled sheath.

Then Merlin told the long-kept secret of his birth, and it was known that he was indeed the son of Utha Pendragon and the rightful High King after him.

So Arthur was crowned by the Archbishop. And after, with Merlin always beside him, he gathered his war-host and in many great battles he drove back the Saxons and the Picts and the men from across the Irish Sea. And when eleven kings from the outlands and the mountain places along the fringes of Britain joined spears and rose against him, he quelled them also, and drove them back into their own mountains. And he made his capital at Camelot, and there he began to gather his court.

Now you must know that Igraine, his mother, had borne three daughters to her first husband before ever she became Utha's queen. And the eldest, Elaine, was married to King Nantres of Garlot, and the second, Margawse, was married to King Lot of Orkney, and the youngest, Morgan La Fay, was married to King Uriens of Gore. And the husbands of all of them were among the eleven outland kings.

Morgan La Fay was a mistress of black magic, and she sought always to do harm to Arthur her half-brother. But it was Margawse who did him the sorest harm in the end. And this was the way of it: she was

9

sent by King Lot, her lord, no one knowing who she was, to play the spy in the High King's court; and she was beautiful, and nearly twice as old as he was, and skilled in the sweet dark ways of temptation; and so she made him love her for one night. Merlin could have warned him, but at that one unlucky time, when he was needed most, Merlin was away about affairs of his own. So the thing happened. And nine months later, back in her own far northern home, Queen Margawse bore a son, whose father was not Lot of Orkney, but her half-brother, Arthur of Britain. And she sent word to the young High King, telling him who she was, and that she had borne their child and named him Mordred, and that one day she would send him to his father's court.

Then Arthur knew that he had done one of the forbidden things, and that because of it, in one way or another, he was doomed. But meanwhile he had a kingdom that must be ruled and a life that must be lived as valiantly and justly and truly and joyfully as might be; and this he set himself to do.

It was not long after that the sword which he had drawn from the stone, and which had served him well in all his fighting since, broke in his hand. And from the Lady of the Lake, he received another sword: the great sword Excalibur, faery-forged for a hero and a High King, which served him all the rest of his days. And a while after that, he saw and loved Guenever, the daughter of Leodegraunce the King of Camelaird, and took her for his Queen.

Guenever brought with her for her dowry a mighty round table and a hundred of her father's best and bravest knights to swell the strength of the High King's own following. And the High King's following was already strong, for champions were gathering to him from the farthest ends of his realm and even from beyond the seas. And so the brotherhood of the Round Table came into being; that great company of knights oath-bound to fight always for the Right; to protect the weak from the tyrants; strong to uphold the ways of justice and gentleness throughout the land.

Merlin saw only the beginning of that gathering, for his own fate was upon him, calling him down to his long enchanted sleep beneath a magic hawthorn tree.

So – the knights gathered, Sir Bors and Sir Lional and Sir Bedivere; from Orkney came Sir Gawain, the High King's nephew (though he was but a few years younger than Arthur himself) and later his brothers Gaheris and Agravane and Gareth, for all the sons of Margawse left her as soon as they could draw sword – all except Mordred. And from the kingdom of Benwick across the Narrow Seas, came Sir Lancelot of the Lake, the greatest of all the brotherhood.

Each of them brought their own story, and men have told and retold them ever since; minstrels singing to the harp in a prince's hall; monks in chilly cloisters writing upon sheets of vellum for the making of books; a Lancastrian knight called Sir Thomas Malory weaving tales and songs together in a narrow prison cell . . . Tales of Sir Lancelot and Elaine the Lily, of Sir Lancelot and the Queen; tales of Geraint and Enid, and Gareth and Linnet, and Gawain and the Green Knight; the long and tragic lament for Tristan and Iseult, the short and shining account of the coming of Percival. These and many and many more together make up the first part of the great story of King Arthur, which I have told in an earlier book, *The Sword and the Circle*.

Only a year after the coming of Percival, there follows the story of the Holy Grail, the cup from which Christ drank at the Last Supper, and which afterwards received His blood; and how the knights of the Round Table set out in quest of the Mystery, for their souls' sake and the sake of the kingdom. And that retelling I have called *The Light Beyond the Forest*.

It is a strange story, of a forest that is not like other forests, and a maimed king and magic ships and a bleeding lance, and always the Grail moving ahead like a beckoning light among the trees.

One by one the knights died in their questing, or lost heart and turned homeward, until only four were left; Sir Percival and Sir Bors, Sir Lancelot and Sir Galahad, his son. And of these four it was given only to Sir Galahad to fully achieve the quest, and in achieving it to die, for mortal man cannot come to the heart of the Mystery and yet live on in the world of men. And Sir Bors and Sir Percival, coming close behind him, achieved something of the quest, and lived on, Sir Percival for a year before he followed Sir Galahad, Sir Bors to return home. And Sir Lancelot, struggling valiantly and desperately behind them, failed the quest because of his love for Guenever the Queen, which he could not put altogether away from him, and so was allowed only a distant glimpse of the glory of the Grail and its meaning before he was turned back.

And so the great days, the shining days of the Round Table were over; and the long, many-coloured, many-stranded story of King Arthur Pendragon turns to its third part; the last and the darkest. The part which in this book I have called *The Road to Camlann*.

2

THE POISONED APPLE

The flowering time that had come to Arthur's Britain with the Grail Quest was over and past, though for a while a golden quietness lingered like the little summer that comes sometimes when the days are growing shorter and the autumn is already well begun.

The knights had returned to sit at their old places at the Round Table – those of them who returned at all. But many of them did not come back, and among them some of the bravest and the best. And a new generation of young knights came in to take their places: men who had never known the early days, the shining days of high adventure, of young champions gathering about a young High King, with the battle to save Britain and champion the Right still in front of them.

And among this wave of new men, his mother Queen Margawse, who had kept him always at her side, being now dead, came Mordred, half-brother to Gawain and Gaheris, Agravane and Gareth. Mordred, who was own son to the High King.

And with his coming, it seemed that the waiting dark began to gather itself, ready for the time of creeping in . . .

Mordred was very like his father to look upon, but cast in a lighter and a slighter mould. Whereas Arthur was brown-skinned, and had been fair-headed like a hayfield at harvest time before his hair became streaked with grey, Mordred had the pallor of something reared in a dark cellar far from the light and air. Pale skin, pale hair, eyes pale and opaque and veined with brilliant blue like turquoise matrix, so that no man could ever see what went on behind them; a voice light and pleasant and somehow pale too. He was a leader of men in his way, though it was not the way of his father, but he could set fashions that men would follow; fashions for wearing black garments, for playing with a flower or a feather between his fingers; a fashion for thinking and secretly speaking ill of the Queen with a shrug of the shoulders and a little laugh.

Mordred had nothing against the Queen herself, but he had not been at court seven days before his subtle mind had divined the love between Guenever and Lancelot, the foremost of the King's knights and his dearest friend, and how the King himself took care not to know, never to recognise, even to himself, that that love existed.

Guenever was the weak place in the King's defences; Lancelot and Guenever together were the way through which he might be reached and brought to ruin, and all that he stood for with him. And Mordred hated his father the High King and coveted his throne, as Margawse, his mother and Arthur's half-sister, had taught him to do through all his childhood and his growing years.

The older and truer knights, Gawain foremost among them, held out against the new fashion. But without anyone knowing how it happened, save Mordred himself, and maybe Agravane the mischief-maker, who from the first was his follower and right-hand man, it was not long before many of the newcomers were whispering among themselves that Sir Lancelot and Queen Guenever were betraying the King by their love for each other, or that Guenever was betraying both of them; and that in any case the King should be told.

For a while it seemed that having raised the small evil wind, there was little more that Mordred could do with it; for Sir Lancelot also heard the whispers, and he said to Sir Bors his cousin, "Now I am thinking it is once more time that I was gone from court for a while."

"That may indeed be so," said Sir Bors. "Yet I think it is no time for one of your far-riding quests, lest when you are far from us and no man knowing where, the Queen may have sudden need of you."

And they looked each other in the eye as old comrades-in-arms, neither speaking Mordred's name. And Lancelot said, "That was in my mind also. Therefore, while the court is here in London I shall go only so far as Windsor, and beg shelter of the hermit there, he that was once of our company, Sir Brassius. None save you shall know where I am gone. But if the Queen has need of me, do you send me instant word."

"That will I," said Sir Bors.

And Sir Lancelot of the Lake donned his armour and sent for his horse and, as he had done to save the reputation of the Queen so many times before, rode away.

And when he was gone, the Queen took to wearing all her jewels and laughing a great deal, to show to all men and women that she cared nothing for Sir Lancelot's going, and was as happy with him far away as she was when he was near at hand. And when he had been gone a while, she made ready to give a private supper party in her own apartments to a few chosen knights of the Round Table.

She bade come to her feast Sir Gawain of Orkney and his brothers Gaheris, Agravane and Gareth, Sir Mordred, Sir Bleoberis the Standard Bearer, Sir Ector of the Marsh and Sir Bors and Sir Kay the Seneschal, Sir Lucan, Sir Mador de la Porte and his cousin Sir Patrice, and a certain Sir Pinel the Wild, cousin to that Sir Lamorack who had been slain in blood feud by the Orkney brothers far back in the years before the coming of the Grail. These and others, twenty in all, the Queen bade to come and sup with her.

And she set herself to order and make ready a feast that should do honour to her guests.

Now all his life Sir Gawain had a great love for fruit, especially apples. This was known to all men and, wherever he was a guest, his host would take pains to see that fruit was set upon the table for his pleasure. So now, though it was late in the year, the Queen took much trouble to come by some of the little golden long-biding apples that are withered and sweet as honey at Christmas, enough to fill a dish to set close by Sir Gawain's place at table.

So then, the Queen held her feast, and those who were bidden to it made merry at her table, while her harper played for them beside the fire of scented logs. But among her guests, Sir Pinel hated the Orkney brothers, Gawain the leader of them most of all, for the sake of his kinsman Sir Lamorack, and for long and long he had brooded upon ways to do them harm; though he had done no more than brood until Sir Mordred came to court. And Sir Pinel also knew of Sir Gawain's love of apples . . .

And when the main part of the feasting was over, the wine still went round, and they fell to eating dried apricots and little honey-and-almond cakes and the like. And then as chance would have it, Sir Gawain and Sir Patrice both reached for an apple in the same instant; and Sir Gawain in courtesy held back his hand for Sir Patrice to take first. And Sir Patrice took the biggest and finest apple from the top of the pile.

If any had been watching, they might have seen that Sir Pinel began a sudden movement of protest, then checked into frozen stillness, staring down at the half-eaten honey-cake in his hand. They might have seen for an instant the trace of a startled frown between Sir Mordred's pale brows, before he took up his wine cup with a faint shrug, as one saying within himself, "Ah well, these things happen."

But nobody chanced to be looking their way.

And Sir Patrice ate the apple to the core, and threw the core into the fire, where it sent up a little hissing spurt of blue flame. And in the same instant he began to choke; and choking and clutching at his throat struggled to rise, then fell sprawling backwards upon the rush-strewn floor.

The men nearest to him sprang to his aid; but he was already dead, and beyond their help.

"Poison!" someone cried.

Mordred, kneeling among those beside the body, remembered small dark hints of his own, dropped into Sir Pinel's ear; remembered also that quickly frozen movement, and knew well enough that the poisoned apple had been meant for Sir Gawain, and who had poisoned it. It would have been better to have had his half-brother Gawain out of the way. Sir Gawain, living, would always be a danger to his plans and was a loyal man to Arthur. But Sir Patrice's death would serve his own purposes well enough, he thought. For the Queen had provided the apples and so suspicion must fall on her – if it were given a little guidance – and with suspicion must come danger; and when word of that danger reached Sir Lancelot, it would fetch him hot-foot back to her aid. Somewhere among all that, though he had no time as yet to see where, must lie the chance to work evil against the King and father whom he hated.

And getting to his feet, he too cried, "Poison!" in a voice of horror, his face turned full upon the Queen.

Then a great uproar broke out in the Queen's chamber, with Sir Mador in the midst of it all, crying that his cousin had been foully slain, and that he would have blood for it, until Sir Gawain shouted him down. "Whoever did this thing, the poison was meant for me, and not for Sir Patrice! All men know the fondness that I have for apples –"

"All men, and all *women*!" shouted back Sir Mador.

"What mean you by that?" demanded Sir Gawain. "Now by God's teeth, speak clear!"

And a second time, into the sudden silence, Sir Mordred whispered, "*Poison!*" as one who cannot believe the horror of his own thoughts, his brilliant blue eyes wide upon the Queen, who had risen and stood as though turned to stone in their midst.

And Sir Mador looked around him at the crowding knights, and said, "I will speak clear! No matter who the poison was meant for, I have lost a kinsman and a friend by it, and in the Queen's apartments. And before you all, I accuse the Queen of his death. Since none but she and her household have had access to the food upon this table!"

And the knights standing all about, Sir Pinel among them, looked aghast at the Queen and at each other. And not one of them spoke up in Guenever's defence, for save Sir Pinel and Sir Mordred there was not one but had suspicion of her in his heart.

And standing in their midst, Queen Guenever began to sway. Soundless and white to the lips, she slid to the ground in a swoon so deep that it was as though she also were dead.

Then while her maidens came running to tend her, word was sent to the King; and he came straightway, and strode in through the doorway just as she sighed and opened her eyes.

"I have heard a wild story," said the King. "Let someone now tell me the truth of it."

And the knights parted, that he might see Sir Patrice lying dead upon the floor. And standing rigidly beside his slain kinsman, Sir Mador de la Porte repeated his accusation against the Queen.

The Queen, who had risen wavering to her feet once more with the help of her maidens, gazed wildly from her lord's face to the face of her accuser. "Before God," said she, "I am innocent of this sin!" and held out beseeching hands.

Arthur crossed the floor and took her hand in his, and holding it, looked about him at his knights. "This is a hideous matter," he said, "but as to your Lady the Queen's part in it, you have heard her swear that she is innocent. Do you accept that?"

"No, my Lord King," said Sir Mador bluntly, "I do not accept it." And no other man spoke at all.

"Then it seems that we must put the case to trial in the Court of Honour," said Arthur. "If I were not the King, I would gladly take my lady's quarrel upon myself and prove her innocence in single combat against all accusers. But I am the King, and so bound by the law to be a just judge and not a champion in any such trial. But, Sir Mador, I make no doubt that another will take my place and give you battle in the Queen's name, rather than that she should suffer death unjustly."

But no knight stood forward to take the Queen's cause upon himself, to prove her innocence in single combat; for to uphold her cause before God's judgement, doubting that it was indeed a rightful one, would be a terrible thing to do, and might set one's very soul in peril.

"My Lord King," said Sir Mador after a long pause, "there is no one here who will fight for the Queen. Therefore name me a day on which I shall have justice."

And with the Queen's hand still strong-held in his, the King said steadily, "Not all the knights of the Round Table are here within this chamber, nor even at court this day. Fifteen days from now, Sir Mador, do you come armed and mounted to the meadows below Westminster. It may be that one will come against you as the Queen's champion; then may God be with the Right. And if none comes, then shall my Queen be ready, that same day, to receive judgement of death upon her."

"I am content," said Sir Mador.

And silently the knights went their separate ways, bearing the body of Sir Patrice among them.

And when the King and Queen were alone, Arthur asked his wife to tell him all she knew of what had happened.

"Truly I know nothing," said Guenever, "but that I had a bowl of apples set for Sir Gawain, and Sir Patrice took the finest apple and ate, and died; and that, before God, I am innocent!"

"That I believe," said the King, "but my belief is not enough. Where is Lancelot, who has been your champion since first he was made knight?"

Guenever shook her head. "Would to God and his sweet mother that I knew; for if I might get word to him, he would surely come and play the champion's part for me now."

The King thought long and heavily. Then he said, "Gawain is too fiery, and the attempt, whoever made it, was on his life . . . Since he cannot fight for you, get word with Sir Bors at once, and ask him – beg him if need be – to do battle for your innocence."

"He is not sure of it," said the Queen. "I saw the doubt in his eyes, like all the rest."

"Beg it of him for Sir Lancelot's sake," said the High King, the words strangling a little in his throat; and he kissed her on the forehead, and turned and strode from the room.

The Queen sent for Sir Bors, and when he stood before her in her chamber, she asked him to fight for her innocence against Sir Mador.

Sir Bors listened to her with a stiff and unhappy face, and said when she had finished, "Madam, how may I do this? I also was at your supper table, and if I now take up your cause, the suspicion of my brother knights will fall upon me also."

"Sir Lancelot would fight for me, were he here," said Guenever, and Bors saw the flicker of hope in her face as she thought of her life-long champion, and he felt, as he had felt it often enough before, that she had played false by both her champion and the King, and so he gave her back harsh words.

"Sir Lancelot might have come as close as Sir Percival or myself to the Mystery of the Grail which he longed for with his whole soul. His love for you cost him that, yet still you would have him back at your call."

Then the Queen humbled herself to Sir Bors, begging him on her knees; and at last he yielded, and swore that he would do battle for her in the Court of Honour if no worthier knight had come forward to be her champion by the fifteenth day.

In the first grey of the next morning, Sir Bors left the royal castle, no man knowing, and rode to the hermitage at Windsor, and told Sir Lancelot of the evil that was upon the Queen. Then he returned to the court, and let it be known by all men that he had sworn to fight in her defence, if no more worthy knight had come forward by the appointed day.

The day of the trial came, and the meadow below Westminster was made ready. The lists were set up, and the stands for the onlookers hung with coloured stuffs as gay as for a Midsummer jousting. But at the upper end of the meadow a tall iron stake stood stark and menacing, with brushwood piled high about its foot, ready for the Queen if Sir Mador had the victory; for death by burning was in those times the punishment for murder, as it was for many other crimes that were all called by the name of treason.

Then the High King came down with his knights about him, and the Queen, well guarded and in the keeping of the Constable and his men-at-arms, walking to her place as proud and seemingly unshaken as ever she had been when she came down with her maidens to watch the jousting among the Round Table knights. Only she took care not to look at the stake and the piled brushwood as she passed them by.

Then Sir Mador stood out before the King, and again made formal accusation against Queen Guenever of the death of Sir Patrice his kinsman. And standing there, he swore that he would prove her guilt, before

God, at hazard of his own life, against any man who came forward to maintain her innocence.

And at that, Sir Bors stood forward to give him answer. "Here I stand in the Queen's defence, to maintain her innocence of this crime, in God's name, unless, even now, a better knight than I shall come forward as her champion."

"The challenge is given and accepted," said the King, looking straight before him, but not at either of them. "Now let the champions make ready."

And the trumpets rang in the wintry air, and both knights turned and went each to his own pavilion, where a squire waited, holding his horse. And in the waiting silence they mounted and rode to the opposite ends of the lists.

As they turned their horses to face each other the winter sunshine struck thin and clear upon the colours of their shields and their horses' trappings and the tips of their skyward-pointing spears. In another moment those spears would swing slowly down into the couched position. But in the waiting pause, three swans came flying up-river, with outstretched necks and musical throb of wings. And the Queen turned to watch them as though they might be her last sight of beauty in this world. But Sir Bors was looking the other way, towards the little wood that bordered the meadow to the north. And as the swans passed on upriver it seemed that the throb of their wings was changed into a beat of another kind, the nearing beat of a horse's hooves.

And in the same instant that the heralds raised their long gilded trumpets to sound for the joust to begin, out from the wood rode a stranger knight on a white horse, and carrying the Virgescue, the plain white shield carried by a new-made knight until he had earned a device to bear upon it – or by a knight who wished to ride unknown.

All eyes were upon him as he headed for the end of the lists and reined in beside Sir Bors. And his voice rang hollow in his helmet, but clear through the wintry air. "Sir Bors, pray you yield me this quarrel on the Queen's behalf, for I have a better right to it than you."

"If the High King gives his leave," said Sir Bors. "Come," and together the two knights rode down the lists to the canopied stand with the red dragon floating flame-like above it, where Arthur sat in the midst of his court. "My Lord King," said Bors, "here is come another knight that would take upon him the defence of the Queen."

Arthur looked at the figure in the plain dark armour carrying an unblazoned shield, and caught the light-flicker of unseen eyes looking back at him from behind the vizor, but nothing more. "Your pardon, sir," he said, "you carry the Virgescue; how then may we judge your fitness for this combat?"

"He is a better knight than I am," Sir Bors said quickly. "Therefore I am freed of my promise."

And the Queen leaned forward a little in her place among the Constable's men-at-arms, watching the newcomer with widened eyes, as she had watched him since the moment that he broke from the woodshore.

The King said slowly, staring straight into that faint eye-flicker behind the stranger's vizor, "Is this true, that you wish to take the proof of the Queen's innocence upon yourself?"

26

"It is for that purpose that I am come," said the knight. And Arthur was sure that he was speaking in a voice not his own, and a small sharp hope began to grow in him that he knew the true voice behind the disguised one. Also he was sure that Sir Bors knew, and would never have yielded up the quarrel to one who was not indeed a better knight than himself.

So he said, "If Sir Mador agrees, then the quarrel is yours to take upon you as the Queen's champion in this Court of Honour –" He checked. Almost, he had said, "And may God give you the victory!" but justice was justice, and he was the King and must uphold it. So he ended, "And may God give the victory to him whose cause is the true one."

And when the thing was put to Sir Mador, who had come from his end of the lists to join them, he said, "It was agreed between Sir Bors and me that we should settle this thing together unless a better knight than he came to take his place. If he swears that this is the better knight he spoke of, then I must accept his word and be content."

So Sir Mador and the unknown knight saluted each other and rode apart to the opposite ends of the lists. Then the trumpets sang, and couching their lances they set their horses to a canter that quickened to a gallop as they swept in upon each other, the clods from their hooves flying up like startled birds behind them.

And as they came together, Sir Gawain said to Sir Ector of the Marsh beside him, "Now I would wager a made falcon against a barley loaf that that is Lancelot. For all the bare shield he carries, I know him by his riding."

For some knights had a way of losing speed in the last instant before the shock, but Sir Lancelot had a way of setting fire to his horse at that same instant, so that at the moment of impact he was travelling faster than the man he rode against; and oft-times that gave him the advantage. So now, as they came together in a pealing crash that echoed across the river meadows, Sir Mador's spear caught at the wrong angle and splintered into three pieces that flew up, turning over and over in the air above them, while the strange knight's spear, travelling like a lightning-shaft, took Sir Mador squarely on the shield and hurled him and his horse together back into a crashing fall.

Sir Mador rolled clear of the threshing hooves, and scrambled to his feet, flinging his battered shield before him and drawing his sword. And the stranger knight swung down from his saddle, tossing aside his spear, and, drawing sword also, charged in to meet him, while squires came running to take his horse and get Sir Mador's to its feet. So they came together, blade to blade, thrusting and traversing, tracing and foining, hurling together as it might be two great boars battling for the lordship of the herd.

The best part of an hour the struggle lasted, for Sir Mador was a skilled and valiant fighter, proved in many battles. But at last the strange knight caught him off-balance, and got in a blow that brought him half to the ground. But even as the stranger stood over him with blade upraised, Sir Mador was afoot again, and in the act of rising, drove his blade into the thick of the other's thigh, so that the blood ran down. The stranger staggered, then sprang in once more with such a buffet to the head that Sir Mador went down

28

full length and all asprawl. The stranger bestrode his body and stooped to pull off his helmet. But Sir Mador cried quarter, in a voice thickened by the blow; and the stranger knight checked his hand.

"Quarter you shall have," said he, "so that you take back all accusation against the Queen."

"That will I," gasped Sir Mador. "From henceforth I will hold her blameless in this matter, and proved so by God's will in trial by combat."

Then the squires came to lift him up and help him away to his pavilion; and the Constable's men-at-arms gladly fell back to give clear passage to Queen Guenever. And the Queen walked out from among them like one walking in her sleep, to where the High King stood under the royal canopy with hands held out to receive her.

And the stranger knight came as custom demanded, halting on his wounded leg, to make his reverence to the King. And King Arthur bent down to greet and thank him, the Queen also, her eyes suddenly very bright in her face that was beginning to wake back to life.

"Sir Knight," said Arthur the High King, "will you not unhelm, that I may see the face of the champion who has saved the life and the honour of my Queen?"

Then the knight pulled off his helmet, clumsy-fingered with the weariness of battle, and thrust back the mail coif beneath. And all men saw under the thick mane of badger-grey hair, the strange, crooked, ugly-beautiful face of Sir Lancelot of the Lake.

"So," said Arthur, and he reached out his free hand to grip Sir Lancelot's mailed shoulder. "Lancelot, my thanks to you, in God's name!"

"Nay," said Sir Lancelot, "no thanks are needed. Have I not been the Queen's champion since the day she belted on my sword?"

And the Queen gave him her hand, as was proper for a queen in thanks to her champion, so that for a long moment the three of them were linked together. And she let the tears that she could not hold back run free and in silence, rather than wipe them away before all those looking on.

Then the squires came to support Sir Lancelot away after Sir Mador, to receive the leech-craft of Morgan Tudd the King's physician.

And the knights came crowding round, voicing their joy at Lancelot's return; and Sir Gawain was shouting, "Did I not say I knew him by his riding?" to anyone who would listen. And Mordred glanced round with a small east-wind smile for Sir Pinel, who had been beside him. But of Sir Pinel there was no sign. Nor was he ever to appear at court again. Mordred shrugged – the man might have made a useful tool. But Lancelot had been netted and fetched back to court; and the Queen's name had been smirched, and though she had been proclaimed innocent by trial of combat, people would never quite forget . . .

Enough harm had been done for that one day.

Sir Mordred strolled back to where the horses waited, smiling faintly, and playing with the peacock feather between his fingers as he went.

3
GUENEVER
RIDES A'MAYING

Sir Lancelot's wound took long to heal. Winter and
spring passed by before he could sit his horse or even
walk without pain. And during all that time he must
remain at court where he might have the leech-craft
of Morgan Tudd. And though the Queen grieved for
his hurt, taken on her account, she thought, "Now at
least he cannot be for ever riding away. Now surely
he will turn, he will turn back to me as he used to do,
before the Grail Quest came between us."

But Lancelot, by putting out all the strength that was in him, did not turn to her again. Instead, he set himself to keep from being ever alone with her, and even to seek the company of other ladies and damosels, though never one above the rest. And as soon as his wound would stand it, he took to riding out by himself, to find sanctuary with the hermit at Windsor or in some other forest refuge.

And gradually the Queen's joy turned cold and angry within her. And when more than a year had gone by, one spring day when the court was at Camelot, she sent for Lancelot to her chamber, and when her maidens had left them alone, she said to him, "Sir Lancelot, I see and feel daily that your love for me grows less. More and more as your wound heals you take to the forest; and even when you are here you turn your face from me and seek the company of other ladies as once you sought mine. Tell me now, and truly, have you taken back your love from me and given it to one younger and more fair?"

Standing before her, Sir Lancelot shook his big ugly head. "My heart lies in your breast, Guenever, as it has done since the day that I was made knight. Surely you must know that. And every time I turn from you I tear at my own heart-strings. But you must know also that there is much whispered talk all about us here at court. And it is so that we must keep apart, lest harm come of it, to you, and to me, and above all to the King." He was silent a moment, fidgeting with his sword-belt, and Guenever silent, watching him. Then he looked up and met her gaze, humbly but straightly. "Also there is another thing, Guenever. Because of my love for you, God denied me what He gave to Percival and Bors when we followed the Grail Quest; and by that I know how deeply sinful is this love of ours, and how it cuts us off from His Grace."

The Queen said, "I wish that I could disbelieve you; for if it were another lady, another love, I could fight her – I could win you back from her as I won you back from Elaine the Lily. But you are hiding from me behind God." She had spoken quietly at first, but her voice grew high and shrill until it cracked in her throat. "And God I cannot fight. Go then, and be at peace with God! You say that you tear your own heart-strings when you turn from me, but do you not see that all this while you are tearing mine?" At the last, she was screaming at him. "Go! Go! Be happy with your God, and never come near me again!"

And as Sir Lancelot turned without a word and blundered like a blind man from the room, she flung herself down sobbing upon the wolfskin rug before the hearth.

So yet again Sir Lancelot rode away; and this time more sorrowfully than ever before, for this was the first time that the Queen herself had bidden him go. But though he disappeared into the forest, not even Sir Bors now knowing where he rode, he was never far beyond a day's ride from Camelot, for in the changed and shadowed times since Mordred came to court he carried always with him an uneasiness lest some new harm should threaten the Queen when he was not by to guard her.

And so, even when she had sent him away, the Queen did not know how faithfully he kept near to her lest she have need of him.

And indeed it was well that he did so, for not many days went by before Guenever did indeed have need of her champion once again.

This was the way of it.

After he was gone, Queen Guenever did as she had done before, donning all her most brilliant gowns and making a great show of gaiety and laughter, that all might see how little it mattered to her whether he stayed or went. And within a little while, on the eve of May Day, she called to her ten young knights of the Round Table, and bade them to ride a'Maying with her on the morrow, into the meadows and woodlands round about to welcome summer in; to hear the cuckoo and bring home the white branches of the may.

"Come well horsed," she said, "and clad all in green as befits the day. And bring each of you a squire with you; and I will bring with me ten of my maidens, that each knight may have a maiden to ride with him, for May is the month of lovers, when no one should ride alone."

So they made ready, and next morning while the dew was still on the grass, they set out, blithe as a charm of goldfinches, and all clad in springtime green, and their horses' harness chiming with little silver bells as they rode. Here and there they ambled and dallied, over the meadows and through the woodlands, singing and calling back to the cuckoo: the knights standing in their stirrups to reach up and break knots of creamy blossom from the hawthorn trees to stick in their caps or give to the damosels who rode with them.

And so, with song and laughter, they rode further and further into the forest.

Now there was a certain knight called Sir Meliagraunce, who at that time held one of Arthur's castles within seven miles of Camelot. And he had loved Queen Guenever in secret for many years. Often he had watched her when she rode abroad, dreaming of ways to carry her back to his own hearth. And on this day, when chance word reached him of how she rode close by, with no armed men about her but only a handful of knights and their squires, unweaponed and dressed in green for Maying, knowing that Lancelot was away from the court, it seemed to him that his chance was come. And all his sense forsook him, and thinking nothing of what must happen after, he called out his whole following of twenty armed men and a hundred archers, and led them down into the wooded valley where the Queen and her company rode, and silently ringed them round, keeping well back among the trees so that they suspected nothing until an arrow thrumming out of a nearby thicket pitched into the ground almost under the muzzle of the foremost palfrey.

The animal squealed and reared, startling those behind him, and for a moment all was confusion. And then as the Queen's knights fought to get their horses back under control, suddenly they found themselves surrounded by armed men on all sides; and out on to the track ahead of them rode Sir Meliagraunce, leather-clad but with his shield on his arm and his drawn sword in his hand.

"Sir Meliagraunce!" said the Queen, startled and not yet fully understanding. "Is this some wild jest?"

"Jesting was never further from my heart!" cried Sir Meliagraunce, striving to thrust his way through the milling horses to her side.

"Then what meaning lies behind this strange and most discourteous behaviour?"

And now Sir Meliagraunce had reached her and grasped her bridle. "No time for courtesy. Come with me now to my castle. I will answer all the questions that you choose to ask, so that you ride with me."

"Traitor!" cried the Queen, trying to pull her bridle free as he wrenched her horse round. "Remember that you are a knight of the Round Table! Will you shame yourself and dishonour all knighthood and the King who made you one of that brotherhood? Me you shall never shame, for I will kill myself before you touch me!"

"Fine valiant talk, madam!" said Sir Meliagraunce. "But I am beyond caring for it. I have loved you these many years, and never before found the chance to gain what my heart desires!"

The Queen's knights had closed up around her and were seeking to drag him from her side, but they had no weapons, and from every side Sir Meliagraunce's armed men thrust in. And though they and the squires with them fought like the bravest of the brave to protect their lady, it was not long before all of them lay wounded upon the ground – though indeed a goodly company of Sir Meliagraunce's men lay sprawled around them.

Then seeing her knights lying so, and the men-at-arms standing over them with drawn swords, the Queen cried out in horror and pity, "Sir Meliagraunce, bid your men to stay their hands! Do not slay my valiant knights who have been brought to this pass through their faith to me! Promise me that, and I will go with you. Promise it not, or fail in your promise, and I will indeed kill myself!"

"Madam," said Sir Meliagraunce, "for your sake I will spare them, and bring them with us into my castle, and see that their wounds are tended, if you will ride with me and smile upon me."

So the wounded knights were heaved again on to horseback, some into the saddle, the more sorely wounded slung across their horses' withers. And with Sir Meliagraunce's hand upon the Queen's bridle, where the little silver bells still rang as though in mockery, they headed for his castle.

But as they rode, one of the squires, less sorely hurt than his fellows, seized his chance as they were fording a stream and, wheeling his horse, struck spurs to its flanks and galloped back the way they had come. Several of the archers loosed after him, but the arrows flew wide, and though some of the men-at-arms spurred in his wake, he soon shook them off among the trees.

"It will be not my questions, but my Lord the King's that you will be answering before long," said Queen Guenever, "and it is in my mind that they will be pressed home with the point of a sword! Better let me free now, and my knights with me, while you may!"

But Sir Meliagraunce was beyond listening; and he left thirty of his best archers posted at the head of the valley, with orders to shoot the horse of any knight who came after them, but on no account to harm the rider – just so much sense was left to him – and still clutching the Queen's bridle, and with the rest of his following close about him, he pressed on with desperate speed towards the castle that he held from the King.

Meanwhile, in the midst of the past night, Sir Lancelot, sleeping among the hounds beside the hearth in a forester's hut, dreamed that Guenever was threatened by some danger and calling for him. He was gifted or maybe cursed from time to time with the power of dreaming true. And he knew the true dreams from those which were but fancy. So when he woke, still in the wolf-dark of the night, he got up, quieting the hounds as best he could, told the drowsy forester that he must be away, and armed himself while the man, grumbling, saddled his horse. Then he mounted and rode away back towards Camelot.

All the rest of the night he rode, as though the Wild Hunt were after him. Dawn paled in the east, and he rode the morning sun up the sky, thundering on through the green and white and gold of May Day morning, until, some while still short of noon, he came up through the steep streets of Camelot town to the gates of the royal castle that crested the hill.

The first person he met was Sir Gawain, who shouted with gladness to see him.

But Lancelot had no time to spare for the joys of friendship. "Where is the Queen?" he demanded.

"She rode a'Maying with ten of the younger knights and her bonniest maidens. They should be back soon enough now," said Sir Gawain, looking into the other's haggard face.

And at that moment they heard more flying hooves coming up the street; and in through the gate, blood streaking his face from the great gash on his forehead, rode Hew, the young squire.

When he had gasped and stammered out his story, Sir Lancelot who had stood fretting with his mail gloves the while, shouted for a fresh horse, and when it was brought, flung himself into the saddle, calling to the King and his knights, who by then were gathering all about, "Arm quickly, and follow me. At Sir Meliagraunce's castle you shall find me if I am still alive. And we may save the Queen!"

And he dashed out through the gate and down the steep narrow street, his horse's hooves striking fire from the cobbles, and on across the river by the three-arched bridge, the cloud of young-summer dust rising behind him, until the sunlit green of the forest gathered him into itself.

Presently he came to a place that showed signs of fighting; undergrowth broken down and bloodstains on the trampled grass; and a while further on suddenly his way was barred by thirty archers, each with an arrow nocked to his drawn bowstring. "Turn back, Sir Knight," said one, who seemed to be their captain, "this way is closed to you."

"By what right?" demanded Lancelot.

"Ne'er mind for that," said the man, "you shall not pass this way, or if you do, it shall be captive and on foot, for your horse we shall slay."

"That shall be of small gain to you," said Sir Lancelot, and striking spurs to his horse, charged them forthwith. Next instant came the twanging of released bowstrings, and a deep drone as of angry hornets, and the horse neighed shrilly and plunged to the ground, a score of arrows in its breast. But Sir

Lancelot sprang clear as the poor brute rolled over, and sword in hand charged upon the archers. But they broke and fled, crashing away into the forest in all directions, so that he could come up with none of them.

Then Sir Lancelot went on his way on foot. But his armour and shield weighed heavy upon him, for full knightly harness was never meant for long walking in, and bore more painfully upon him with every spear's throw of distance that he covered. And beside this, the wound in his thigh, that he had got when he fought Sir Mador de la Porte for the Queen's innocence, though it was long-since healed, had left him with a leg that was not yet fully serviceable, and the weight and the chafe of his armour upon it began to irk him so that he could make less and less of speed, while all the while the dark taste of last night's dream was with him, Guenever in danger and calling to him – calling and calling. Yet with the kind of welcome he was like to meet at Sir Meliagraunce's castle, he was loath to cast any of his harness aside.

But by and by he reached a track, and along the track towards him came a cart driven by one man, with another sitting on the side of it with his legs dangling.

A sudden flicker of hope woke in Lancelot. "Hi, good fellows!" he shouted. "What will you take to drive me in your cart to a castle not two miles from here?"

"Nay, you'll not come into my cart," said the driver, "for I'm heading the other way, to fetch wood for my lord, Sir Meliagraunce."

"It is with Sir Meliagraunce that I have business," said Sir Lancelot grimly.

"Then you can go and find him on your own two feet." The driver would have whipped up his bony nag and driven over the knight in his path, but Sir Lancelot sprung on to the bow of the cart, and as the man turned his whip against him fetched him such a clout on the side of the head with his mailed fist that he tumbled down from his perch like a stoned bird, and lay still.

Then the other man cried out, "Fair lord, spare my life, and I will drive you wheresoever you would go!"

"You know already where I would go – and that swiftly!" said Sir Lancelot, climbing into the cart. And the carter scrambled forward to take the reins.

"Sir Meliagraunce. Aye, you shall be at his gate before you can count to ten," said the man, already heaving the horse and cart around. Then he set off up the track, rattling and lurching at such a speed as the old horse had not made for many a long year.

In the Great Chamber above the keep of Sir Meliagraunce's castle, Queen Guenever waited with all her maidens about her, and her wounded knights and squires upon the rush-strewn floor. For she had demanded to have all her people with her, that she and her maidens might tend their wounds, and also that Sir Meliagraunce might have no chance to come upon her alone.

And one of her maidens, watching from the window, called suddenly, "Madam, come and see – there is a cart coming up the track, and a knight standing in it. Poor knight, he must be going to his hanging!" (For no man of armour-bearing rank would ride in a cart unless on his shameful way to the gallows.)

41

"Where?" said the Queen, and looking from the window she beheld the wood-cart, and the knight riding in it; and she knew with a knowledge of the heart, even before she could make out the device on his shield, that it was Sir Lancelot. "Nay, that is no knight riding to a felon's death," she said, "though indeed he must be hard put to it, that he comes to my rescue in such a manner." And to herself she said, "Yet I knew that he would come – despite all things, I knew that he would come."

And as she watched, the cart drew up before the castle gateway, and Sir Lancelot sprang down and shouted in a voice that set the hollow gate-arch ringing: "Open the gates, Sir Meliagraunce, false knight of the Round Table and traitor to your liege lord Arthur. The High King and his company are not far behind me, but first stand I, Sir Lancelot of the Lake, ready to do battle with you and all your following!"

And he hurled himself at the little wicket within the great main gate, which in haste and panic had not been made properly secure, and burst it open and came charging through the knot of gate-guards inside, striking out right and left as he came, like a boar that breaks loose and charges with the hounds snapping about his flanks.

When Sir Meliagraunce knew that Sir Lancelot was within his gates, panic rose in him, and he bolted up to the Great Chamber and cast himself down at the Queen's feet, crying, "Mercy, madam! Pray you have mercy on me, for I was driven to this madness by my love for you!"

"It is not for me to have mercy," said the Queen, "but for the knight who comes to rescue me, and for my lord the High King, who I doubt not follows hard after."

"You can speak for me!" howled Sir Meliagraunce. "Tell them I have done you no harm, but used you with all courtesy –" And he tried to cling to the hem of her green skirts.

"Certainly you have used me with more courtesy than you have used my poor knights," said the Queen, and drew back her skirts from his clinging hands.

"I was mad!" wailed Sir Meliagraunce. "Only speak to Sir Lancelot and the High King for me, and I will serve you humbly in whatever way you choose!"

"Cease this outcry, and get up," said the Queen at last, "and I will speak to them for you, that they spare your life; for truly peace is better than war."

And she went to meet Sir Lancelot as he came storming in search of her. And when they met they went for an instant straight into each other's arms. "I knew that you would come," said the Queen against his shoulder. "Despite all, I knew that you would come to save me!"

And Sir Lancelot said, "I dreamed you were in danger. I heard you calling me, and so I came."

And then he pulled away from her, demanding, "Where is Sir Meliagraunce?"

"In the Great Chamber," said the Queen, suddenly mid-way between tears and laughter, "and very sore afraid!"

"He has cause to be," said Sir Lancelot, "for now his death is upon him."

"Nay! I have promised him that I will cry your mercy for him, since what he did, he did for love of me!"

And they moved further apart from each other, touching only with their eyes.

But after, Guenever took Sir Lancelot by the hand and led him up to the Great Chamber where were her maidens and the wounded knights and squires; and Sir Meliagraunce still kneeling, who looked at her with eyes like a beaten dog. So, slowly and with much labour and persuasion, she made a kind of peace between Sir Lancelot and Sir Meliagraunce, though even then it was agreed that they should fight the matter out in single combat that day week, before King Arthur in the jousting meadow below Camelot.

And hardly was that settled before the High King himself and his knights were in the castle courtyard.

And Guenever made peace also between them and Sir Meliagraunce on the same condition of single combat, for the King upheld Sir Lancelot, agreeing that no vengeance should be taken upon Sir Meliagraunce nor upon any of his people, but that day week should end the matter. "But if either fails to keep his tryst," said the King with a stern eye upon Sir Meliagraunce, "then shall he be called craven ever after, and the shame of all Logres."

That night they remained in the castle that Sir Meliagraunce held from the King; and next morning, with the Queen in their midst, and those of the wounded knights who were too sick to sit their horses borne in litters, they set out to return to Camelot. But when Sir Lancelot would have departed with the rest, Sir Meliagraunce came to him, smiling, and making great show of friendliness, and said, "Gentle sir, the Queen has made peace between you and me, until the day comes that we settle this matter by weapon-skill for the honour of us both. But pray you tell me of your own accord that you feel no ill will towards me in the meantime."

"None in the world," said Sir Lancelot, shortly.

"Then do you prove it, by remaining here as my honoured guest until the day of combat comes."

Sir Lancelot looked at the man's humbly smiling face, and scorn rose in him, and he felt sick. He would have liked to strike him; but Sir Meliagraunce was so small inside himself, and seemed now so contemptibly and pitifully eager to please, and Sir Lancelot was ashamed of his own contempt. So he said as warmly as he could manage, "I thank you for your courtesy, and most gladly I will stay here with you until we ride for Camelot together."

And so, after the rest had set out, he remained behind with Sir Meliagraunce.

Later that day his host asked Sir Lancelot would it please him to see the hawks in his mews, especially a very fine jerfalcon that he had lately had brought to him from the islands of the North. And Sir Lancelot, who loved falconry and always trained his own birds, said that it would pleasure him greatly. But as they went down to the inner courtyard which contained the mews, Sir Meliagraunce stood aside at a doorway for Sir Lancelot to pass through ahead of him. And Sir Lancelot, passing through, trod on the spring-board of a trap cunningly concealed in the floor; and the trap opened beneath his feet and he fell twice the height of a man into a vault deeply floored with straw.

And Sir Meliagraunce made the trap secure again, and went on his way, heedless of the muffled shouting beneath his feet.

*

In Camelot time went by towards the appointed day of combat. And on the last day of all, there came to Arthur's court a certain young knight out of Hungary, called Sir Urre. A most potent knight he had been with his heart ever set on adventure; but he came in sore need of help, lying weak and forespent in a horse litter, and his mother and sister riding with him.

They were brought in and made welcome as honoured guests. But the King spoke to Sir Urre's mother apart. "Most welcome are you and your son and the damosel your daughter to my court; but tell me, lady, why you have brought him so far from his own place to mine. Sick and weak as he is, so long a journey must have been grievous hard for him to bear."

"Hard indeed; and long indeed the journey," said the lady, and he saw that she must have been fair to look upon before sorrow came to her; but now she was haggard and weary, and there was a wild and seeking look in her eyes. "Seven long years ago my son, who sought adventure and high deeds even more than most young men, was in Spain, and there in a great tournament he fought with one, Sir Alphegus, and slew him, but received from him first seven wounds, three in the head and three in the body and one in his sword-hand. It was a fair fight, but the mother of Sir Alphegus cursed him for her son's death; and she was one who had power from the Devil in her. And by her black powers she so wrought that my son's wounds should bleed and fester without healing and he should never be whole again until his wounds were searched by the best knight in the world.

And so for seven long years we have travelled through all the lands of Christendom, seeking the best knight in all the world; but to no avail; and if we do not find him here, I fear me that my son will never be whole again."

"Take heart, lady," the King said kindly, "for here in Britain – in Logres which is the brightness at the heart of Britain – your son must surely be healed of his wounds, for there are no better knights in Christendom than are gathered about my Round Table."

But as he spoke, he wondered. Once, he would have known that that was true; he prayed that it was true still, but he could no longer be sure.

But now, with the wounded knight lying there in his pain and weakness, and the lady's anguished and beseeching gaze fixed upon his face, was no time to be listening to such doubts in his heart. "I myself will be the first to lay hands upon your son," he said. "Well I know that I am not worthy to work this miracle; yet I am the High King, and if I go first, that shall give courage to my knights to follow me. For you must know well, madam, that this is no light thing that you ask of us."

Then he knelt down beside Sir Urre, whose litter had been taken from its horse-shafts and laid upon the floor of the Great Hall. "Sir Knight," he said, "I grieve for your suffering. Will you allow that I touch your wounds?"

"Do as you will with me, my Lord King," said Sir Urre, his voice dry and weary in his throat; but it was clear that he had lost all hope of healing at any man's hands.

Then the linen bandages were laid back, and the

47

King touched Sir Urre upon each of the seven sickening wounds. But though he was as gentle as might be, the sick knight clenched his teeth, and winced at every touch. And when he had touched them all, the seven wounds were just as they had been before.

"I knew that it would not be I," said the King, "but pray you be of good courage; there are better knights by far than I am, here in my court."

Then one after another all the knights that were there at court came forward to lay their hands upon Sir Urre. Sir Gawain and his brothers, Sir Lional and Sir Bors and Sir Ector of the Marsh, Sir Bleoberis, Sir Kay the Seneschal and Sir Meliot de Logure, Sir Uwaine, Sir Gryflet le Fise de Dieu, Sir Lucan and Sir Bedivere, Sir Mador and Sir Persant of Inde – and Sir Mordred, at whose touch the wounded knight could not forbear a groan. And many others, a hundred or more. And when the last had tried in vain, Sir Urre was near to swooning with the pain and weariness of so many hands upon him. Yet his wounds were all unchanged, save that they bled the more from so much handling.

"Now we sorely need Sir Lancelot of the Lake," said King Arthur.

"Aye, well, he will be here tomorrow," said Gawain, "when he comes with Sir Meliagraunce to keep their day of combat."

Meanwhile Sir Lancelot had lain six days and six nights prisoned in the vault below Sir Meliagraunce's castle, and every day there came a maiden who opened the trap and let food and drink down to him on the end of a silken cord. And every day she whispered to him, sweet and tempting, "Sir Lancelot, oh, sweet Sir Lancelot, I will bring you free out of this place if you will be my lord and my love."

And every day he refused her, until on the last day her anger rose and she said, "Sir Knight, you are not wise to spurn me, for without my help you will not win free of this captivity. And if you are still here at noon tomorrow, your honour will be gone for ever."

"It would be greater dishonour for me to buy my freedom at your price," said Sir Lancelot, "and the High King and all men know me well enough, I hope, to know that it is not cowardice but some mischance or treachery against me that could hold me from keeping my tryst when the appointed day of combat comes."

And the maiden secured the trap again and went her way.

Next morning, lying in the dark and listening to the sounds of the castle that filtered down to him from overhead, Sir Lancelot heard Sir Meliagraunce ride away, his horse's hooves ringing hollow on the court-yard cobbles and out through the gate arch to the lower court. And he beat his fists together in fury and despair. But soon after, the maiden came, and lifted the trap, and knelt weeping beside it, looking down at him, while he stood below her looking up. And she said, "Alas! Sir Lancelot, I had hoped to win you, but you are too strong-set against me, and my love for you has been in vain. Yet I cannot see you dishonoured. Give me but one kiss in guerdon, and I will set you free, and you shall have back your armour, aye, and the best horse in Sir Meliagraunce's stable."

"There is no harm in a kiss," said Sir Lancelot. "It is but courteous to thank a lady for her kindness."

Then the maiden sent down a good stout rope with knots tied in it, in place of the silken cord. "I have made the end fast to the bar-socket of the door," she said. "Trust me, it will bear your weight. Now climb."

And Sir Lancelot swarmed up the rope, and standing beside her when she had made all secure again, he kissed her once. Only once, but long and tenderly, for he was a man to pay his debts. Then the lady brought him to the armoury, and served him as his squire, aiding him to put on his armour, and when he was armed, and his sword at his side and a spear in his hand, she took him to the stables, where twelve fine coursers stood in their stalls, and bade him choose whichever he would.

He chose one that was as white as milk, with an arched neck and a falcon's eye, and she aided him to saddle and bridle it, for the grooms, like everyone else in the castle, had gone streaming away after their lord to Camelot.

And in the lower court he mounted, and leaning down to her from the high saddle, said, "Lady, my thanks are yours for all time; and all my life my service is yours if you should need it, for this day's work."

And touching his spurs to the horse's flank, he clattered out under the gate arch, while the maiden stood looking after him with the taste of her own salt tears on her lips where his kiss had been, as other maidens had stood before her.

Sir Lancelot settled down into the high saddle, and set his horse's head towards Camelot. He had seven miles to cover before noon, and the time was short, with the sun already high in the sky.

Meanwhile in the meadow between the town and the

river, all things had been made ready for the joust. The King and Queen and all the court had come down to watch; even Sir Urre had been borne down to the field on his litter and set in the shade of a clump of ancient alder trees. And Sir Meliagraunce had already arrived. And when the King, seeing that he rode alone, asked for Sir Lancelot, he showed great surprise. "Sir Lancelot? Is he not here? He left me on the morning of the second day, to ride off on some business of his own; but I did not think that he would forget this day – unless . . ."

"Unless?" said the King.

"Unless, maybe, having been so long accounted the Queen's champion and the best of knights, and being no longer so young as once he was . . ." said Sir Meliagraunce, and grinned under the shadow of his open vizor.

"That sounds not like Sir Lancelot," said the King.

And Sir Gawain standing close by growled into his rusty beard, "And he that says so speaks foul slander! If Sir Lancelot comes not to keep this day, it is slain or wounded the man is – or lies captive somewhere!"

And if any had been looking at the Queen, they would have seen how her face faded to the whey-white of thorn blossoms.

But no one was looking at the Queen, for at that moment the sun flashed back from some point of swiftly moving light across the river, and upon the waiting quiet came the urgent beat of a horse's hooves, and craning that way they saw a knight on a white destrier come pricking out of the forest on to the river track. He headed for the three-arched bridge and came drumming over; and as he drew near, and they made out the device on his shield, the shout went up, "It is Sir Lancelot! It is Sir Lancelot of the Lake!"

And if any had *then* been looking at the Queen, (but no one was, save maybe Sir Mordred) they would have seen her flush from her whey-whiteness to a painful fiery rose.

Sir Lancelot swung left-hand from the bridge on to the tilting ground, and reined to a trampling halt, his horse scattering foam from its muzzle.

Then the King sent squires to summon Sir Lancelot before him. And Sir Lancelot set his horse pacing forward up the field and reined in again, below the stand where the King sat with Guenever the Queen at his side.

"Sir Lancelot," said the King, "you come late to your tryst."

And Sir Lancelot spoke up in a loud clear voice for all the company to hear, and told how Sir Meliagraunce had dealt with him in the past days. And Sir Meliagraunce would have turned his horse and been swiftly on his way; but the King checked him. And he sat by, with a frightened and sullen face, and could make no answer when King Arthur demanded of him whether he could deny the charge.

Then Lancelot said, "My Lord King, this creature who calls himself a knight, and a knight of the Round Table, has sought by treachery to bring black dishonour upon my name; therefore, in place of the simple joust which was planned for today, I demand that he shall do battle with me to the uttermost." Which was to say, to the death, neither man being free to yield himself to the other's mercy if he were defeated in the usual custom of a joust.

52

"The demand is granted," said the King.

Then a fresh horse was brought for Sir Lancelot, and he and Sir Meliagraunce drew apart to the far ends of the lists, and turned, and at the trumpet's sounding, set their spears in rest, and came thundering down upon each other. And Sir Lancelot's spear took Sir Meliagraunce in midshield, and hove him backwards over his horse's crupper.

Then as Sir Meliagraunce scrambled to his feet, Sir Lancelot swung down from his horse; and drawing their swords, they fell to hewing and smiting at each other, until at last Sir Lancelot got in such a blow to the side of his adversary's helm that he went down like a poled ox.

But Sir Meliagraunce scrambled towards Sir Lancelot and clung to his knees, crying, "Spare my life! I yield me! I cry quarter and yield me to your mercy!"

Then Sir Lancelot did not know what to do, for this was a fight to the uttermost, and he was bound for his honour's sake neither to ask nor to give mercy, but to kill or be killed. Yet his gorge rose at the thought of killing a man grovelling at his feet.

"Get up!" he said. "Get up and fight, if you would not shame your manhood more than you have done already!"

But the other went on grovelling and clinging and crying out, "I yield! I yield! Spare my life!"

"*Get up!*" said Sir Lancelot in an agony. "And I will lay aside my helmet and my shield and my left gauntlet and fight you with my left hand tied behind my back!"

Then Sir Meliagraunce ceased howling, and stumbled to his feet and cried out for all to hear, "My Lord the King, take heed of this offer, for I will accept it!"

53

There was a sick silence, and then a murmur of distaste among the watching knights, and the King said to his friend, "Sir Lancelot, are you set upon this?"

And Sir Lancelot said steadily, "I never yet went back on my word."

So the squires came and took his helm and shield, and bound his left arm behind his back; and the two knights stood once more face to face; and a murmur ran round the field at sight of Sir Lancelot standing there bareheaded and shieldless and one-handed, before his fully-armed opponent. Then Sir Meliagraunce swung up his sword, and Sir Lancelot stood as it were drawing him on with his bare head and shieldless left flank; then as the blade came whistling down, he side-slipped and twisted with a silver flash like a leaping salmon, swinging up his own sword Joyeux so that the two clashed and ground together and for a moment hung locked. And then the other blade was beaten aside, and Sir Lancelot's blade took his enemy on the helmet-crest with such force that both the helmet and the head within it were cloven in two, and Sir Meliagraunce fell dead upon the trampled ground.

Then the squires came and bore his body away, leading his horse after it. And while Sir Lancelot stood leaning on his sword and wiping the sweat out of his eyes with the back of his bare hand, the King himself went to him and led him to where Sir Urre lay upon his litter under the alder trees. And he told Sir Lancelot of the knight's wounds, and how they had all failed to heal him.

"And indeed," said Arthur, "we had small hope of success, seeing that his wounds may be healed only by the touch of the best knight in Christendom. But now that you are returned to us, the hope rises again within our hearts."

"In mine also," said Sir Urre; and his eyes clung to Sir Lancelot's face like the eyes of a sick dog. And his mother and sister were standing by.

"Not me," said Sir Lancelot, "this is for the best knight in Christendom. God forbid that I should think to achieve what so many good knights have failed to do!"

"It is for the best knight in Christendom," the King said gently.

Sir Lancelot shook his head. "I was, maybe, once."

"Galahad is dead," said the King, still more gently. And then, "See now, you do this thing not out of any pride or presumption, but because your King commands you."

"Then I must obey the King's command," said Sir Lancelot. He was weary to the bone, and still rank with the sweat of battle. And he knew that if he tried to do this thing, and failed, he would be shamed before all his fellows of the Round Table. But he knelt down beside the litter, and set his hands together, one bare and the other still mailed, and prayed deep in his own heart where none might hear him save the One to whom he prayed, "Oh God, make me your servant and your channel for the healing of this sick knight. By your virtue and grace, let him be made whole through me, but never *by* me."

And then, seeing that he still wore his right-hand gauntlet, he stripped it off, and asked Sir Urre very humbly, "Will you grant me now that I touch your wounds?"

55

"In God's name lay your hands upon me," said Sir Urre.

And Sir Lancelot touched the wounds upon his head. And as he did so, it seemed that something flowed through him, like a wind or a fire or his own heart's blood. And the bleeding ceased beneath his hands, and the edges of the wounds drew together. And then he touched the wounds on Sir Urre's body and again the power and the love flowed through him and the wounds closed; and lastly he took Sir Urre's sword-hand in both of his, and felt it grow whole and strong again between his palms.

And he knew that at long last, with all his sins upon him, God had granted him the miracle he had prayed for all his life.

Sir Urre sat up, and looked about him in great wonder, then got slowly to his feet. And King Arthur and all his knights cried out in joy; and kneeling, bowed their heads and gave thanks to God for His mercy.

But kneeling still beside the empty litter, Sir Lancelot covered his face with his big swordsman's hands, and wept like a little child that has been beaten.

4
THE QUEEN'S CHAMBER

Time went by, and on the surface it seemed still that life stood at summer; but below the surface, the shadows were closing in on Britain. The shining light of Logres shone as high and clear as ever, but as a candle flares before it gutters out.

And more and more Sir Lancelot found himself remembering Sir Tristan, dead these nine years past. Sir Tristan sitting beside the fire in the Great Hall at Camelot, his little harp on his knee, turning the love between himself and Iseult of Cornwall into a harp-song of such piercing sorrow and sweetness that all his listeners wept to hear. For more and more Sir Lancelot's love for Guenever was becoming what Tristan's for Iseult had been, a power that dragged him where it would, as the moon drags the tides to follow it.

And always Sir Agravane and Sir Mordred watched him and the Queen, with hatred in their hearts for both of them and for the King also; the King above all, though they made pretence that all their concern was for his sake.

One evening when another May had come round, and again the cuckoo was calling in the wooded hills about Caerleon where the court was at that time, Sir Gawain and his brothers and their half-brother Mor-dred were talking together in the chamber high in the North Tower of the castle where Gawain had his quarters. It was a dark, austere room, with no beauty in it save for the flames upon the hearth and the yellowish-white skin of a great snow-bear with chunks of amber for eyes, that lay slung across the low bed-place. The four Orkney brothers were gathered about the hearth, while Mordred stood by the narrow window, a little removed – he never forgot, nor allowed them to forget, that he was no full brother of theirs – and played with a tiny jewelled dagger as though it were a flower between his fingers.

"We have all seen them together," said Sir Agravane. "We all know how often they are together, and more closely so when we do not see. The whole court knows of their love for each other; and it is foul shame that we should leave the King unwarned."

"The King knows!" said Sir Gawain harshly. "Do you think he is a blind fool?"

Gaheris said, puzzled, "Then why does he do nothing?"

Sir Gareth said slowly, thinking the thing out as he went along, "Do you not see? He knows, but he pretends even to himself that he does *not* know, because so long as he does that, he need do nothing to harm the two people he loves best in the world."

"Well thought out, little brother," said Gawain, "but there's more to it than that."

Sir Agravane said shrilly, "And meanwhile they bring shame upon the King and our Round Table brotherhood, and upon the whole Kingdom of Logres!"

Sir Gawain kicked a smouldering log on the hearth and watched it burst into flame. "There are others who do that," he said, and glared at his brother. "Leave it, Agravane."

"You are the eldest of us, you should tell him."

Rage and helplessness rose in Gawain and almost choked him. He could think of no way out, no way of thrusting back the evil. Even if he were indeed to tell the King – warn him – that would be to do Mordred's work for him, in the end. "I will have no part in it," he growled in his throat. His grey-streaked red hair seemed almost to rise like the hackles of an angry hound. "If you do this, you will tear the Round Table asunder, for you must know that many of the knights will take sides with Sir Lancelot, while others will follow you and Mordred, thinking that in doing that, they stand true to the King – until in your own time you will stand forth against him yourselves. There will be red war, and the end of Logres and all that we have striven for so long. And who will be for the King then?"

"You will be for the King," said Gareth, "and I."

"I also," said Gaheris, "and a few more. Most of us old hounds with grey muzzles."

Sir Mordred spoke for the first time, playing with the dagger. "Agravane, if you are afraid to come with me to the King my father, I will go to him alone."

"Nay, I go with you," said Sir Agravane. "The time has come when our liege lord must be forced to know, and to *act*!"

And a sideways, lip-licking glance passed between him and Mordred.

They turned together and left the room.

The three left by the fire looked after them. "There is no more that we can do," Gawain said. "God's teeth! Even if we were to silence them this way" – he touched the dagger in his belt – "their deaths would force the thing upon Arthur's notice, and so bring the splitting of the Round Table as surely as their telling what they have to tell will do. But wae's me, the darkness comes crowding in, my brothers."

Mordred and Agravane found the King alone in his council chamber, sitting in his High Seat with the dragon-head foreposts and staring at nothing. And kneeling before him as two just men who loved him and could bear to see him wronged no longer, they told him that Lancelot and his Queen were lovers.

The King heard them out in silence. Only his hands clenched more and more fiercely on the carved dragon-heads. The thing that he had always prayed would not happen was happening. He was being forced to know about his wife and his best friend; and from that must come not only darkness for the three of them, but darkness and ruin for the Kingdom of Logres.

But he would not yield to the darkness without fighting. When they had done, he rose slowly to his feet, unfurling all his great height like a banner. He had come, as the years went by, to stoop a little under the burden of his own height, as many tall men do; but he did not stoop now. He stood looking down at them as they knelt still at his feet; his nephew and his ill-begotten son.

"Have a care how you make that accusation," he said. "For once it is made, one or the other of you must prove it in the Court of Honour, against Sir Lancelot himself. It would not be the first time that he has fought for the Queen's innocence; and let you remember the end of that fight. And remember also the time that he fought Sir Meliagraunce with neither shield nor helmet and one hand bound behind his back, and yet Sir Meliagraunce was carried dead from the field."

Agravane said with hurried eagerness, "But if evil-doers are caught in their evildoing, seen by trustworthy witnesses so that the case is proved against them past all doubt, there is no need left for trial by combat."

And Mordred, his voice smooth as silk of Damascus, put in "That is the law, my lord father."

And Arthur felt the trap closing in on him, for all his life he had striven for a world in which people obeyed the laws instead of relying always on the strength of their own sword-hands. He had striven also to make one law for all people, whether they be knight or swineherd or sewing-woman or the Queen herself.

"If you were to ride hunting tomorrow – a two days' hunt with a pitched camp for the night between . . ." Agravane went on.

And the King said quietly, but in a voice that grated in the back of his throat, "You feel that I should turn my tail and slink away until the foul work is safely done?"

"No such thought was in our minds, my lord father," said Mordred in the same silken tone. "But it is only when you are away that Lancelot and the Queen come together. If you refuse, you will be standing of a purpose against the working of *your own law*!"

And Agravane thrust in, "Do you ride hunting tomorrow and let it be known that you will not return until the day after." His narrow face flickered with malice. "So, the Queen will send for her peerless Lancelot, as she has done often enough before. Then we will gather witnesses, and for love of you, that you be no longer shamed, dear Uncle, we will take him in the Queen's chamber, and the thing will be proved."

"And the Queen will be burned and Lancelot beheaded," said the King.

Mordred said gently, "It is the law."

The King was silent, staring down at the two kneeling before him, while his thoughts raced in his head. They were right, as such rightness went; and there was nothing that he could do. But Gawain? The Orkney brothers were too close-bound in love and hate for their chief to have no awareness of the game they hunted. Surely he would warn Lancelot. "Dear God," he prayed in the inmost places of his heart, "there is nothing that I can do, but grant that Gawain warn Lancelot of the danger!"

Aloud, he said, "So be it. Gather your trustworthy witnesses, and take Sir Lancelot of the Lake in the Queen's chamber if you find him there – and if you can. I hope, as I have hoped for few things in my life, that he will kill you both, and your witnesses with you! You have my leave to go from my presence."

So next morning early the King sent for his hounds and horses, and rode hunting with a few companions, leaving word that he would be gone until the evening of the following day. And he bade neither Lancelot nor Gawain to ride with him.

But Sir Gawain could not have ridden on that day's hunting in any case. Ever since the wound that Sir Galahad had given him while they both rode upon the Quest of the Holy Grail, he had suffered at times from woeful pains in his head. At times of stress or sorrow the pain came upon him; and then he would drink to ease it. And so the pain came now, and he felt as though his head must fly in two, and he drank to ease the pain, more than usual because the pain was worse than usual, and fell into a dead sleep. And so he did not warn Sir Lancelot. And Gaheris and Gareth were both with the King's hunting party away in the greenwood chasing the lightfoot deer.

The first day of the King's hunting went by, and at Caerleon, as the warm dusk of early summer stole up from the river meadows, it seemed that shadows of another kind were closing in on the King's castle.

That night, Sir Lancelot sat late in his chamber talking with Sir Bors over a jug of wine. And as they sat, someone passed along the corridor outside the door, a page maybe, and whistling very softly an old tune from the hills of Wales.

Sir Lancelot raised his head to listen, and when the whistler had gone by he got to his feet and wrapped his long furred gown more closely round him, for the castle corridors even on a May night were chilly.

"Finish the wine, my cousin," he said. "I go to speak with the Queen."

Sir Bors said, "Take my counsel, and do not go tonight."

"Why not?" demanded Sir Lancelot, his hand already on the latch.

"Because there is a dread on me," said Bors. "Because Sir Mordred and Sir Agravane watch you too closely, and it is not good to be watched by those two. Because the King is away this night, and I smell danger . . ."

"Have no fear," said Sir Lancelot, "I shall but go and speak with the Queen a little, and come back before you well know that I have gone."

"Then God speed you," said Sir Bors, "and bring you safely and swiftly back indeed."

And then as Sir Lancelot lifted the door latch, he called him back. And Sir Lancelot checked, half-smiling and half-impatient, "What now?"

"Take your sword," said Sir Bors.

Sir Lancelot hesitated a moment then, leaving the door ajar, turned back and took his great sword Joyeux from the carved chest on which it lay. And carrying it under his arm, muffled in the furred folds of his mantle, he went out and through the dark passageways of the castle to the Queen's chamber.

One of Guenever's ladies waited to let him in, then slipped out, closing the great door behind her. And he checked a moment to drop the bar into its wrought-iron socket, which was a thing he had seldom done.

Honey-wax candles burned in the Queen's chamber, and the moonlight slanted in through the high, deep-set windows. And in the mingled apricot-gold of the candles and buttermilk-white of the moon, the Queen stood humming softly and happily to herself, the same tune from her own hills that had sounded outside Sir Lancelot's door, while she poured wine from a silver flagon into the golden cup set with little dark river-pearls that she kept for her most joyous occasions and her best loved people. She looked up when Lancelot came in, and set the flagon down on the top of the beautifully painted chest below the window; and stood holding the cup and smiling at him as he came towards her.

The mingled light fell on her hair, which was un-braided and lying loosely on her shoulders. Guenever's hair was not like Lancelot's, that had turned grey at the time of his wild-wood sickness when he was but twenty-six years old; nor like Arthur's which looked as though he had raked ashy fingers through the mouse-fairness of it. But single white threads shone here and there among the rest that was as black as ever it had been.

"Come and sit you, and drink," she said.

He came, and they shared the cup between them; and sat, she in her great cushioned chair and he on the end of the painted chest, linking together their little fingers in the way of a young squire and his maiden, and talking quietly, content for a while just to be in each other's company, for they had been lovers so long that at times they were like an old wedded couple.

But they had been only a short while together when there came a jangling tramp of mailed feet outside, and a savage beating on the door, and the voices of Sir Mordred and Sir Agravane and of others behind them, shouting for all the court to hear, "Sir Lancelot! Traitor knight! Now are you caught in your treachery!"

Lancelot and Guenever sprang to their feet. "Alas," whispered the Queen, "now we are both betrayed!"

Lancelot looked hurriedly about him. "Those are armed men outside. Is there any of the King's armour here in your chamber? If so, they shall have a fight to remember!"

The Queen shook her head. "I have no armour here, nor any weapon. So now do I fear our long love is come to a bitter end."

"Nay, for I have Joyeux," said Lancelot. And with the uproar still going on like hounds baying for the kill beyond the door, he caught her into his arms and kissed her once, quick and hard. "As I was ever your true knight, pray for my soul if I be slain." Then flinging off his thick mantle he wound it round his left arm to serve for a shield, and drew his sword and turned to the door.

By now the men outside had brought a heavy bench from the Hall to serve as a ram, and the stout timbers were shuddering beneath its blows. "Cease this tumult," he shouted, "and I will come out!" But to the Queen he whispered, "When I have the door shut again, do you put up the bar, for I shall not be able to hold it long, and my hands will be full with other matters."

Then, as for the moment the makeshift ram ceased its crashing, he took his stand just behind the door, setting his left foot behind it so that it might open no further than to let one man through; and sword in hand, he flung back the bar. The door flew back against his foot, and Sir Agravane shot through the opening; and Sir Lancelot forced the door shut and stood braced against it, while the Queen in frantic haste thrust home the bar in the face of the knights outside.

Agravane whirled about with a cry, and aimed a great blow at Lancelot; but Lancelot side-sprang, light without his armour, and took only the glance of it on his muffled left arm; and before his enemy could recover, dealt him a blow to the side of the neck that felled him on the instant, his head half off his shoulders.

"Now help me with all speed!" said Sir Lancelot; and while the door leapt and juddered against its bar, and the baying from outside broke forth afresh, "Traitor knight! Come out from the Queen's chamber!" the high voice of Sir Mordred rising over all, he and the Queen with frantic speed stripped off the dead knight's armour and Sir Lancelot dragged on such of it as was of most use and most quickly donned, the ringmail shirt and the helmet, and caught up Sir Agravane's shield.

"Come out and face us! Out, Sir Traitor!"

"Cease your uproar! I am coming!" shouted back Sir Lancelot. "And as for you, Sir Mordred, my counsel is that you run far and fast before I come!"

And dragging back the bar, he flung open the door and strode out among them. Then, in the narrow passageway and at the stairhead across from the

Queen's door, there was the clash and flash of weapons, half seen where the taperlight gleamed from the Queen's chamber into the dark; and man after man went down before the onslaught of Sir Lancelot of the Lake, tripping each other's trampling feet in the corridor, or pitching backward down the stair, until at last all twelve of those who had followed Sir Mordred and Sir Agravane lay dead as Sir Agravane lay within the Queen's chamber; and Sir Mordred with an arm dripping blood had fled away from the fighting into the night.

Then Sir Lancelot turned back into Guenever's chamber, where she stood like a queen carved in stone for laying on a tomb.

"Come with me," he said.

But she answered, scarce moving even her white lips, "No. I am the King's wife, I must stay and bear the Queen's part. Enough of evil has been done this night."

Sir Lancelot stood for a moment more, breathing heavily and dabbing at a gash on his wrist, his gaze on Guenever's face. Then he said, "It must be for you to choose. If danger comes to you out of this, remember that Bors and Lional and my brother Ector will stand your friends. And if I live, I shall be back."

And he stumbled out into the dark, through the shambles beyond the door.

He managed to regain his own chamber unseen, and found Bors still waiting for him.

"Did I not warn you?" said Sir Bors, as soon as he realised who it was in Sir Agravane's harness.

It was in Sir Lancelot's heart to say, "Yes. And you were right, always you are right; it is one of the

least likeable things about you." But there was no time.
In as few words as might be, he told what had happened,
while he snatched up his own helm and shield in place
of those he bore. "Do you and Lional and Ector stand
friends to the Queen until I return," he said, buckling
on Joyeux. "No harm can come to her under the law
for seven clear days; and if I live, I will be back before
then."

"Where do you ride?" asked Bors.

"To Joyous Gard," said Sir Lancelot, "to gather
my own men."

They looked at each other, a long, bleak look, and
so parted.

That night two men rode through the moonlit dark
as though the Wild Hunt were after them. One was
Sir Lancelot, taking the familiar tracks northward
through the Welsh hills to Joyous Gard; and the other
was Sir Mordred, with an arm swaddled in bloodstained linen, making for the King's hunting camp.

It was at the grey cock-light of dawning when
Mordred reached the camp, and the King was already
up and sitting on a tree-trunk with his head in his
hands, his eyes red-rimmed in the haggard face of a
man who had not slept all night.

When Sir Mordred half fell from his horse and
came and stood before him, he looked up, and seeing
the bloodstained linen and the grey face lit by pale
eyes that blazed with malice, said wearily, "So you
found him, in the Queen's chamber."

"There we found him," said Sir Mordred. And he
told the King from beginning to end of Sir Agravane's
death and the fight outside the Queen's door.

"Did I not say that Sir Lancelot was a matchless knight?" said the King. "Grief upon me that now he is my enemy, after the long years that he has been my dearest friend. Now the Round Table is broken apart for all time, for many of my best knights will hold to him in this matter. Now also, the Queen must die. I should be grateful to you, son Mordred, for the tender care that you have taken of my honour."

And he bent his face again into his hands, and rocked himself as one in sorest pain; then sprang to his feet and shouted for his horse and his gear, and for the camp to be broken, for they were riding at once for Caerleon.

And so, at Caerleon, before the gathered council of his knights, in the presence of the Archbishop, and with clerks to write all down, it was ordained according to the law that Sir Lancelot should be beheaded if he were taken, and the Queen should be burned at the stake, for their unlawful love and for the deaths of Sir Agravane and the twelve knights.

Sir Gawain sought by all means in his power to gain mercy for them, but all to no avail.

"Do not you be over-hasty in this," said Sir Gawain, with his head still ringing with the effects of the drink and the old wound. "For though indeed Lancelot was found in the Queen's chamber, why should it not be as the Queen herself swears – that she bethought her suddenly that she had never thanked him truly for her rescue at his hands from Sir Meliagraunce, and so sent for him to make that matter good?"

"After a year?" said the King, looking straightly at his nephew. And it seemed that deep within him something was crying out, "Why did you not warn them? In sweet Jesus's name could you not have warned them?" But aloud, he said only "Nay, they must suffer as the law decrees."

"Then at least leave the sentence a while before it is carried out."

"Until the seventh morning after it was passed," said the King. "And not a morning longer. That is for the Queen; and for Lancelot, whenever he be captured."

But the truth was that he dared wait no longer, lest he weaken, and so bring to nothing the rule of law that he had fought all his life to establish in Britain.

"Then God grant that I be not by to see it," said Sir Gawain.

"Why so?" said the King. "What cause have you now to love Sir Lancelot or the Queen? For her sake he slew your brother Agravane."

"Often enough I warned my brother Agravane," said Sir Gawain, standing hunched and stubborn as an ox in the furrow. "For well I knew what his ways would bring him to in the end. Moreover, they took Sir Lancelot fourteen against one, which is no fair fight. I will take up no blood feud for Agravane."

But the King let the sentence stand.

And the days went by until it was the eve of the Queen's appointed death-day.

And then the King sent for Gawain to the Great Chamber high above the keep, where he was pacing up and down like a caged beast, and bade him make ready his finest armour, to take command next day of the escort that should bring Queen Guenever to the fire. "For after Sir Lancelot, you are the Captain of the Round Table, and the thing is for you to do," said he.

"Yet I will not do it, my uncle and my Lord King," said Sir Gawain, "for I will not stand to see her die, nor will I have it ever said that I was with you in your council for her death."

And looking at him, the King knew that Sir Gawain would die himself before he changed from that. So he sent for Gaheris and Gareth and gave them the same commands. "Do you both take command of the escort, and between you see the Queen securely guarded lest Sir Lancelot come to attempt her rescue." For an innermost voice within him said, "Surely Lancelot will save her, even now," while another said, "Yet that must not be, for if he rescue her and carry her away, and live, then indeed there will be civil war in Britain!" And between the two, it seemed to him that he was being torn asunder.

The two younger knights looked at him in horror; and Gareth said, "Sir Lancelot knighted me!"

And Gaheris said, "He saved me from Sir Tarquine, and always he has stood as a friend to me!"

"Nevertheless, you shall obey the orders of your king," said Arthur, and his voice grated in his throat.

They stood rigid before him, and Gareth was grey-white, as though he himself were being ordered to the stake. But they had sworn fealty to the High King, and the habit of obedience and discipline was stronger in them than ever it had been in Gawain. And at last Gareth said, "If that is your last word, then we must obey your orders, my liege lord, but we will not take up arms against Sir Lancelot, but go forth unarmed and in robes of mourning that the Queen may know to the end our love towards her."

"I am with my brother in this," said Sir Gaheris.

"In the name of God then, make you ready, and go forth in whatever guise you choose," cried the King.

And Sir Gawain with the tears trickling into his red beard, said "Grief upon me, that I was born to see this day!" And he turned and stumbled away to his chamber, his two brothers following.

And the King returned to his caged pacing up and down.

Next morning the Queen was led forth to the open space beyond the castle walls, where the stake waited for her with brushwood piled around its foot. And her queenly garments were stripped from her so that she stood up only in her white shift. And a priest was brought to confess her that she might be shriven of her sins. And then she was led towards the stake, and lifted up upon the pyre, and bound there above the heads of the people. And all the crowd who had gathered there in sorrow or in triumph fell back, so that only her escort remained near at hand; and the two figures in their darkly hooded cloaks of Sir Gaheris and Sir Gareth.

And the King stood watching from the high window in the keep, as rigid as though he too were bound to a stake. And he never saw the blink of light three times repeated from the tower of the old church opposite, in the instant that the Queen was brought out from the castle; for all his gaze was fixed upon the open space below.

73

A great quiet had fallen over the crowd, and the executioner's torch was already lit. And the King was listening for something, listening with an aching intensity that seemed to hold his very heart in check. And then he heard it – the drum of horses' hooves, far in the distance but sweeping nearer at full gallop.

Riding day and night, with many changes of horse along the way, Sir Lancelot was back from Joyous Gard, with his own fighting men behind him. Everybody knew that it was Sir Lancelot; the youngest weeping page and the executioner pausing, torch in hand, the High King in his window, and the Queen bound to her stake. They knew, even before the bright arrowhead of horsemen burst out from the narrow ways between the houses into the crowded square. He and his men had lain up in the woods overnight, while one of their number in an all-concealing cloak had entered the town and kept watch in the church tower, to signal with the sunlight on his shield the moment when the Queen was brought out clear of the castle walls.

The mailed arrowhead of horsemen drove into the crowd and through it, the early sunlight jinking on their weapons and harness; and the shouts and cries and weapon-clash and the trampling of horses' hooves came up in a surf-roar of sound to the King in his high window; and below him the fight swirled about the pyre, small with distance but terrible. The executioner's torch had gone down, to be trampled out beneath the horses' hooves. He saw Lancelot's blade rise and fall in desperate, slashing strokes, as he forced his tall destrier through to the pyre, and again the flash of Joyeux's blade, this time slashing through the cords that bound Guenever to the stake. Far below, he saw the Queen hold out her white arms to her love, as Sir Lancelot reached from the saddle to fling a dark cloak around her. How like Lancelot, he thought, to remember that she would be stripped to her shift, and bring a woman's cloak with him. Next instant he had caught her from her footing among the piled brushwood and dragged her across his saddlebow. Then, holding her close, swung his horse round and with his own men closing all about him, was fighting his way out.

And then it was over, and the hoof-beats drumming away into the distance, no man following. And in the square below the castle walls the crowd were in a turmoil, and round the unlit pyre men lay dead on the stained and trampled ground. And still the High King stood as though captive in his window, torn between despair for what he knew must now come to Britain, even as Merlin had foretold, and a sick relief that Lancelot had saved the Queen.

A strange blackness came between him and the scene down in the square, between him and all the world, so that for a while he saw nothing more. But when the world came back to him again, he was still standing in the window, but holding to the deep stone transom, his forehead pressed down against his hand. And hurrying footsteps were blundering up the stair and into the chamber. He straightened himself from the window and turned, and found Sir Gawain standing before him, staring at him with blazing eyes in a terrible grey face.

Gawain said, choking on the words, "He has killed Gareth and Gaheris!"

75

"Who?" said Arthur. His head felt numb and would not think.

"Sir Lancelot! He has killed Gareth and Gaheris! They are lying down there by the scaffold with their heads split open."

The King shook his own head. He could not believe it; it must be that there was some mistake. "Not Gareth. Not Gaheris either. He loved Gareth best of all the Round Table after you – and me."

"They are lying down there with their heads split open," Gawain repeated; and it was as though he must fight to get enough breath to speak the words. "Lancelot killed them unarmed."

"Unarmed," the King said quickly, "and in those grey-hooded cloaks. He would have had no means of knowing them."

"Gareth was by half a head the tallest of your knights!" said Sir Gawain. "By his height alone, no man could have failed to know him . . . I would not take up the blood feud for Agravane, but I take it up now for Gaheris and for Gareth. And I will not be laying it down again so long as the life is in me – or in Sir Lancelot of the Lake!"

And he flung himself down on a bench, his head in his arms, and wept gaspingly and agonisingly for the the death of his brothers; and for the old love between himself and Lancelot that was now turned to hate.

And standing unnoticed in a corner, gentling his arm in its sling, Sir Mordred, who had come up behind Sir Gawain, smiled like one well content with the skilled work of his hands.

5
TWO CASTLES

Sir Lancelot carried the Queen away through the mountains to his own castle of Joyous Gard. And there he lodged her with all honour, as befitted Arthur's Queen.

And at Joyous Gard there gathered to him Sir Ector of the Marsh, his half-brother, and his kinsmen, Sir Bors and Sir Lional, and many more, upward half of of the Round Table, both for his sake and the Queen's.

And King Arthur would fain have let all things rest a while, that hot blood might have space to cool, and time might sort out the good from the evil. But those knights who were still of his following, Sir Gawain foremost among them, were at him night and day, that Sir Lancelot was his enemy and had carried off his Queen, and he should make war upon him as he would upon any other foe within his borders. And so at last the High King sent out the summons to all his war-host; and marched upon Joyous Gard.

Sir Lancelot had word of their coming, and knew that it was Sir Gawain more than the King who was against him; for Sir Bors and the rest had told him of how he had slain Sir Gaheris and Sir Gareth, and warned him of what must follow. That had made bitter hearing, for he would have hacked off his own right hand before he knowingly did harm to either of them. But the *mêlée* about the stake had been too fierce to leave time for singling out two unarmed men among the surging press of knights and men-at-arms, nor for choosing where his sword-strokes landed, nor for noticing that one dark-hooded figure was taller than all the rest about the stake. He had had no time or thought for anything but cutting his way through to save the Queen. But truly, after Gawain and the King, he loved Gareth best of all the Round Table brotherhood; and his heart seemed bleeding within him for their deaths at his hand. Now there was blood feud between him and Sir Gawain, and grief for that tore at him also. But there was no time for bewailing what had come to pass, with the King's war-host marching north against him.

So he gathered his fighting men and called in all the folk of the valley and the village beyond the gates, and their cattle with them, and penned all safe within the castle walls, and made ready in all ways that were possible. And the King came and pitched his war-camp below the walls of Joyous Gard, so that all the valley round about was fluttering with the pennants of his nobles and their knights. And he laid siege to Joyous Gard.

For fifteen weeks the siege dragged on, while the summer passed, and the fields along the valley floor were white with barley and golden with wheat, and the great ox-wagons should have been bringing in the sheaves that the horses of the King's war-host trampled down. But the castle was strong and well-garrisoned and still well-supplied, and at the end of that time it was no nearer to falling than it had been on the first day.

And then on a day towards the edge of autumn, Sir Lancelot spoke from the ramparts with the King and Sir Gawain sitting their great warhorses below him in the open stretch between the walls and the camp.

"My lords both," said Sir Lancelot, "you will gain no honour in this siege. You have sat here long and long, but you will not take Joyous Gard."

"And you will gain no honour skulking behind castle walls," flung back the King. "Do you come out and meet me in single combat, that we may end this matter. I swear that no other shall be with me."

This was the thing of all others that Sir Lancelot had dreaded, and the chief reason why he had held back so long. "God forbid," he said, "that I should encounter with the most noble king in Christendom, and he my liege lord from whose hands I received my knighthood."

"Out upon your fair language!" cried the King, beside himself with grief that he could only bear by turning it into anger. "Know this, and believe it, that I am your enemy and always shall be; for you have slain my knights and borne away my Queen, and broken asunder the brotherhood of the Round Table and the Kingdom of Logres."

"The slaying of your knights, alas, I cannot deny," returned Sir Lancelot, "and among them those that were dear friends to me, for which the grief will be upon me all my days. But it was done in the saving of the life of your Queen, whom you condemned to the fire. From that fire it was, and not from you, that I bore the Queen away, as I have saved her from other dangers before now, and received thanks from both of you." And he leaned further out over the parapet and demanded, "My Lord King, look in your heart – would you indeed have had her burn?"

"Shut your treacherous mouth!" shouted Sir Gawain, half-mad with fury, before the King could answer. "Have done with this twisting of the truth; for all men know the shame of what lies between you and the Queen!"

Lancelot answered him in a lion's roar. "Do you accuse the Queen, then?"

"Nay, I speak no word against the Queen. On you lies the guilt, the false treachery to your liege lord –"

"That is well for you," Sir Lancelot flung back at him, "for I will fight for the Queen's innocence as I have done before, against any man save the King. And if I come out against you, Sir Gawain, beware of my coming!"

And he turned and strode away down the rampart stair, with a parting insult from the man who had so long been his friend, ringing in his ears.

And the King, with Lancelot's question "Would you indeed have had her burn?" sounding still in his own heart, wheeled his horse and rode back to the royal camp in silence, with Sir Gawain cursing and half-sobbing beside him.

Within the castle, Sir Bors and Sir Lional and Sir Ector and the rest came to Lancelot and said, "It is time for fighting! We who love you know that it is for love of the King that you have remained so long behind these walls, hoping for peace between you. But the King will make no peace with you; not while Sir Gawain stands at his shoulder. And to bide longer within walls after the insults that have been flung at you this day will look like fear to men who do not know you as we do. Fight now, for your right and your honour, and we are your men!"

And Lancelot knew that they spoke truth; and knew also, that with the harvest lying wrecked and un-gathered, the stores within the castle must soon be sinking low.

So next morning the gates and sally-ports of the castle were flung open, and with trumpets sounding and spear-head pennants fluttering many-coloured over all, Sir Lancelot led out his knights and squires and men-at-arms to the fight.

Then from the King's camp the trumpets crowed in reply, as fighting-cocks send their challenge one to another at dawn. And the King and his knights rode out to meet them; and the two companies rolled together like two great waves, and crashed upon each other; and all the open land below the castle was a'swirl and a'trample with battle, and the end-of-summer dust-cloud rising and billowing over all.

The whole day they fought. And in the thick of the fighting Sir Gawain, seeking Sir Lancelot, came up against Sir Lional across his way, and ran him through the body so that he dropped dead from the saddle. And Sir Bors, seeing what befell, and charging to avenge his brother, hacked down Sir Gawain, and then came shield to shield with Arthur himself. For a few straining and sweating moments they grappled together, their swords locked at the hilt, like the still centre at the heart of a whirlpool, among the surge of men and horses all about them; and then Sir Bors broke his blade free, and fetched the King a blow that pitched him down into the bloody dust under the trampling hooves of the battle. Sir Bors, plunging out of the saddle, stood over him with drawn sword, and a little gap opened as the fighting shifted, and Sir Lancelot was there.

Sir Bors shouted to him, "Shall I make an end to this war?"

"Not in *that* way, unless you would lose your own head," said Sir Lancelot grimly. "For I will not see my liege lord either slain or shamed while I stand by!"

And he dismounted also, while Sir Bors, still sword in hand, stood back; and he helped the King to his feet again, and mounted him from his own knee back into the saddle of his snorting and trampling horse.

"My most dear lord," he said, "for Christ's sweet sake let us end this strife. Take back your Queen – so that you take her with love and honour, letting no more harm come to her. And I will cross the Narrow Seas to Benwick, and return no more, unless the time comes that you have need of me."

"The law –" said the King, drooping in his saddle. "The Queen is not above the law – but must be as any poor woman –"

"And that you have proved. But mercy is above the law. Can you not give her your mercy, as you might give it to any poor woman?"

And the King looked down into the ugly, haggard face of the knight standing at his stirrup, and the love that he had had for him and for Guenever the Queen swelled within him until it seemed that his heart must burst through his rib-cage. And he said, "Bring the Queen to me in tomorrow's morning, and she shall have all honour, and her place beside me again, and my love as she has had it all these years."

And Sir Gawain had been carried from the field to have his wounds tended; so the truce was made, and the two armies drew apart.

A little later, straight from the battle and without waiting to disarm and wash off the sweat and the blood as at other times he would have done, Sir Lancelot went to the Queen in her chamber.

"Is the fighting over?" she asked; for she had not dared to climb the keep stair and watch, for dread of what she would see.

"The fighting is over. It *must* be over," said Sir Lancelot heavily. "Gawain has killed Lional – and many other good knights are slain. And for my sake Bors would have slain the King, if I had not stayed him."

And the Queen looked into his face, and at what she saw there she gave a low cry and held out her arms to him.

83

But he drew away. "Nay, I am still foul from the battle-field."

"What have you really come to tell me?" she asked; and gestured her women from the room.

And Lancelot told her what had passed between himself and the High King.

She heard him through in silence; and when he had done, she said, "The glove for me and the sword for you. Do you remember Tristan and Iseult?" And then she said, "How if I will not go back?"

"You must go back," said Sir Lancelot. "Did I not tell you, Sir Bors would have slain the King for our sakes? If you return to him and take your old place, and if I go back to Benwick, then it may be that the wound that splits the Round Table apart and threatens all Logres will heal."

"And we shall never see each other again," said Guenever.

"And we shall never see each other again," said Lancelot.

"God help us both," said the Queen. "For we shall surely need it." And she pressed close to him, heedless of his battle-foulness and the harshness of his war-gear through the thin stuff of her gown. And she took his strange face between her hands and kissed him, once on the forehead and once on the mouth, and turned away to let him go.

Next morning early, the gates of Joyous Gard were opened wide, and Sir Lancelot, all unarmed and leading the Queen by the hand, came out. And behind him all his knights, unarmed likewise and bearing green truce-branches robbed from the castle garden. And so he led her to the King where he stood, his own nobles behind him, under an ancient hawthorn tree in the midst of the camp.

Then Sir Lancelot and the Queen knelt before the High King, and Sir Lancelot said in a loud clear voice for all to hear, "My liege lord the High King, I bring here to you the Lady Guenever, your Queen. Mine alone is the blame if aught has been between us that should not have been; for she is as true to you as ever was lady to her lord; and if any knight dare to say otherwise, I stand ready to prove her innocence in single combat to the death!"

As he finished speaking, his gaze seemed drawn past the King, and for a moment it caught and locked with the pale gaze of Sir Mordred, who stood with a cluster of young knights a little to one side. And in that moment Sir Mordred smiled. His small silken smile made the gorge rise in Sir Lancelot's throat. But he spoke no word, and the King's son only went on playing with the late blood-red corn poppy between his fingers.

It was Sir Gawain who spoke first; grey-faced and red-eyed, with a bloody clout round his shoulder. "I have said it before; I speak no word against the Queen. The King must do as he chooses in this. But between you and me, for my two brothers' sake, there is blood feud, and I am your enemy while the breath is in my body – or in yours."

And the King stooped, still speaking no word, for at that moment he could not, and lifted the Queen to her feet.

Lancelot rose, and stood before his king, his head up, and his hands clenched under the folds of his cloak. "And now, my Lord the King, I take my leave of you, and of this land where I gained my knighthood and all that ever I have had of honour. I am for the south coast, and my own lands of Benwick across the Narrow Seas."

"You have fifteen days," said King Arthur.

And Lancelot said, "The King is generous. It was only three that King Marc of Cornwall gave to Sir Tristan in like case."

And in the minds of both of them was the old sorrowful story told by Sir Tristan himself beside the fire in the Great Hall at Camelot on that wild All Hallows' Eve so long ago. And they could have wept each on the other's neck.

Again it was Gawain who broke the silence. "Wherever you go, see that your sword sits loose in its sheath, for I swear that I will come after you!"

"No," Lancelot said, "do not swear, do not come after me. For God's sake, do not hound the King into coming after me. Let the war end and its wounds heal over."

Then he turned to Guenever, who stood white and watching at the King's side; and said clearly and proudly and again for all to hear, "Madam, now I must leave you and my fellows of the Round Table for ever. Pray for me in the years to come, and if ever you have need of one to fight for you, send me word, and if I yet live, I will come."

Gravely and distantly, he kissed her hand; then turned away, leaving her with the King.

He did not look back, nor did she follow him with her eyes, though it seemed that this was the last time that they should see each other in the world of men.

Indeed, there was to be one time more, but there

would be little of joy in that meeting, for either of them.

So Sir Lancelot rode south through dust-dark forests beginning to flame with autumn, until he came to the coast. And there he took ship across the Narrow Seas, and so returned to Benwick and his own people. But he did not go quite alone. Most of the knights who had gathered to him at Joyous Gard returned to King Arthur's court and their old allegiance; but his half-brother Sir Ector of the Marsh, and his kinsman Sir Bors and a handful more, headed by old Sir Bleoberis who had been King Utha Pendragon's standard-bearer when he and the world were young, went with him or followed after. And in Benwick the knights and lords of his own following gladly welcomed him back.

The autumn and the winter passed, and for a while it seemed that there was peace in Britain. But Sir Gawain never for a breath of time forgot or forgave the death of his brothers; and day and night he urged the King to gather his forces and go after Sir Lancelot and finish the war indeed.

"For it was never truly ended," said he, "but only broken off midway. And so long as Lancelot sits lordly in his own domains, there will be knights to slip away to him whenever any ruling of yours displeases them."

"Remember Sir Bors and Sir Ector, and others beside, are with him even now," said Mordred gently and regretfully. "And he has his own knights to gather to him also." And he spoke of rumours that Sir

Lancelot was gathering a war-host. And once it was gathered, what should it be used for, save for making war on his liege lord? And if ever Sir Gawain showed any sign that his wrath was cooling, Mordred would drip a little more poison into his heart to make the wound break out afresh. And the King was no more the man he had been. Something of his strength was gone, and of his faith in himself and his own judgement. Something seemed broken within him; maybe it was his heart. And so he listened to Sir Gawain whom he loved, and to Sir Mordred whom he tried not to hate, when he should have listened to the voice within himself. And when the year turned again to spring, he began gathering his war-host; and the land rang with the sound of armourers' hammers; and ships were made ready and lying in south coast harbours, waiting to ferry men and horses across the Narrow Seas.

And when the seafaring weather of early summer came, Arthur led his war-host across to Benwick, to carry forward the war against Sir Lancelot to its bitter end.

And behind him he left Sir Mordred to govern the kingdom during his absence, and to protect the Queen. His loyal knights were aghast at his decision, and full of dread. But the King had a sense of Fate upon him. He knew deep within himself that the pattern was almost finished; and the doom upon himself and all that he had fought for, which he had unleashed when he fathered Mordred on his own half-sister, was hard upon him; and maybe he would hold out his arms to it rather than seek to fend it off, seeing that there was no escape. No escape from the doom, no escape from the ordained end of the pattern . . .

"He is my son," he said, "he has something of my own gift for leading men. And there is no one else."

So then, the High King left his son behind him and took his war-host across the Narrow Seas, and led them through the lands of Benwick until they reached its great castle. And they made their camp before the castle and laid siege to it, as they had done to Joyous Gard.

Then the knights who were with Sir Lancelot begged him to lead them out at once, to give battle. "For we were bred and trained up for honourable fighting," said they, "not for cowering behind castle walls."

"First I will send word to the King under the green branch," said Sir Lancelot, "for still I am bitter loath to fight my liege lord; and peace is always better than war."

And he sent a maiden mounted on a white palfrey with a branch of green willow in her hands into the King's camp, to see whether peace might not be made once more between them.

But with Sir Gawain beside him, the King would not listen to her plea; and so the maiden returned weeping to Sir Lancelot.

And scarcely had she told of her failure, than Sir Gawain, mounted on his proudest warhorse and with a mighty spear in his hand, was before the main gate shouting, "Sir Lancelot of the Lake! Is there none of your proud knights dares break spear with me?"

"I claim first spear in answer to that!" said Sir Bors. And he made ready and rode out to encounter Sir Gawain; and when they set their spears in rest and charged together, Sir Bors was unhorsed at the first shock and sorely hurt, and must have been lost, but that a band of knights charged out to his rescue and carried him back into the castle.

And next day Sir Gawain came again, and this time Sir Ector answered his challenge; and he also was felled, and borne back by his rescuers within the gates.

And the siege lasted many months, and again and again Sir Gawain came with his challenge. And it seemed that no champion could stand against him; for every knight who rode out in answer to his challenge he slew or wounded, and took no scathe himself. And then one day, sear and chill on the very edge of winter, Sir Gawain came yet again, and cried out, his great voice rough and echoing within his helmet, "Are you listening, Sir Lancelot, traitor and coward? Or have you hidden your head beneath the pillows? Come out now and give me combat, or carry the shame for ever! For here I wait to take my vengeance for the death of my brothers!"

And Sir Lancelot could bear it no longer; and he bade his squires to harness and bring round his best horse, and he rode out to answer Sir Gawain's challenge. "God knows it is with a heavy heart I join battle with you, Sir Gawain, both for the old friendship between us and because you are blood-kin to the High King, but you drive me to it, so now must I turn upon you as a boar turns at bay!"

"This is no more the time for words," said Sir Gawain. "Now you shall give me satisfaction for my brothers' slaying; and there shall be no breaking-off between us while the life remains in us both."

Then they drew their horses far apart, and turning,

couched their lances, struck in their spurs and came thundering down upon each other, while from the King's camp and the walls of Benwick Castle men looked on with the breath caught in their throats. They came together with such a rending crash that both horses and riders were brought down in a struggling tangle. The champions rolled clear of their horses and stumbled to their feet, drawing their swords, and fell to, thrusting and smiting and foining until their armour was hacked and dinted, and their blood ran down to spatter the trampled grass like the small crimson flowers that the people in eastern lands used to call the Tears of Tammuz.

And at last Sir Lancelot fetched Sir Gawain such a blow on the helmet that the blade bit through and made a great wound in his head beneath, in the place where the old wound had been, so that he might not rise again. And Sir Lancelot drew aside and stood gasping for breath and leaning on his sword.

And Sir Gawain cried out to him in an agony, "Now slay on! For I swear that when I am whole I shall do battle with you again!"

"That must be as it will," said Sir Lancelot, "but I never yet slew a felled and wounded knight in cold blood; and sweet Jesu knows the blood is cold within me this day!"

And he turned and limped wearily away, while men from the royal camp came out and bore Sir Gawain, still raving, back to the King's pavilion, where the King's own physician Morgan Tudd waited to salve his wounds.

And the siege dragged on, and the wild geese came down from the North to winter in the marshes nearby and there was ice along the edges of the tracks. And so soon as Sir Gawain could sit firm upon his horse he was back at the gates of Benwick Castle, crying like a madman for Sir Lancelot to come out to him. "For the last time we fought, by some mischance I had sore hurt at your hands, so now I come to take my revenge, and lay you as low as last time you laid me!"

"Now God forbid," said Lancelot to his knights, "for then I think that my time would be short indeed!"

But he called for his horse, and rode out. And again they fought, and again after long and desperate struggle, the battle ended as it had done before; and by evil chance the final blow of Sir Lancelot's sword fell yet again upon the selfsame place as the old wound. And Sir Lancelot, walking with a sick heart back towards his castle gates and his knights assembled there, heard behind him a terrible sobbing and gasping voice that cried after him, "Traitor knight! Traitor knight! When I am whole again . . ." and then ceased as Sir Gawain sank into a deep swoon, and the men from the King's camp bore him away like one that is dead.

Sir Gawain lay for many days near to death and raving, while the siege dragged on through the chill and sodden winter, and the King's men endured as best they could under canvas or in the wrecked and empty town. And it was the edge of spring, with the days lengthening and the first catkins showing yellow on the hazel thickets, before Sir Gawain could sit on his horse once more. But as soon as he could bear spear and shield, his first thought was to ride out and challenge Sir Lancelot yet again; for now he seemed to have no room in his poor wounded head for any thought except this one.

But on the very eve of the day when he would have ridden out again, despite all that the King or his fellow knights could say to hold him back, news came from Britain that ended the siege.

6

THE USURPER

Left to govern Britain while the flower of the Round
Table fellowship slew each other beyond the Narrow
Seas, Sir Mordred was soon about the next part of
his plans. His gift for setting fashions had become the
gift for leading men, which his father the High King
had known that he possessed. Already he had his
following among the younger knights, and as the
summer passed and turned to autumn, and then the
winter went by, others who had never truly been
Arthur's men gathered to him at Camelot; and the

men of the North and beyond the Irish Sea began to creep back, sending in their leaders to speak with him behind closed doors, drawn by rumours of easier terms and a looser rule than ever they had had from Arthur Pendragon. Word began to go round too – no man knowing who started it – that if Mordred and not Arthur were King, the taxes that they had to pay for the safe-keeping of the realm would somehow be lighter, and the strong laws that he had made would be slackened. Men began to prick their ears, and those who were still true to the High King in their hearts were uneasy and bewildered, not knowing what they were supposed to do. And the whole realm began to grow unsure.

Guenever knew a little of what was going on, but she kept herself close in the women's quarters these days, rather than mingle with the new company at court; and she prayed with a heart full of dread for Arthur's return and for peace between the sundered halves of the Round Table, and that Arthur's return might not mean that Lancelot was slain.

The feast of Candlemas went by, and there were snowdrops in the castle's high-walled garden, and then the first short-stemmed primroses along the river banks below the town. And a day came; a grey shivering day that had none of the hope of spring in it, but a little moaning uneasy wind that made strange whisperings along the corridors and stirred the tapestries on the walls of the Queen's bower, where she sat at her embroidery with one of her favourite maidens.

When she was young she had worked fair and light-hearted things with her needle; a unicorn, milk-white on a background sprinkled thick with pinks and heartsease pansies, with birds and butterflies among the leaves overhead. And later she had worked the proud red dragon of Britain upon golden damask, to make a shield-case for the High King. Now she was working angels with spread wings upon an altar hanging for the castle chapel. She had not the gift of prayer. Though she prayed long and often in these days, she knew that her prayers never truly took wing; so she embroidered the angels with their spread wings of gold and crimson and violet, with some half-hope that they might carry her prayers upward; or even that God might accept them as another kind of prayer. "See, I am doing this for you. You who can do all things, pray you save Arthur – pray you save Lancelot – pray you save Britain from the dark."

It was drawing in towards evening; soon it would be time for the pages to bring the honey-wax tapers. She could scarcely see to set the fine stitches any longer. She turned her embroidery frame to catch the last fading daylight from the western window. And as she did so, she was suddenly aware of distant sounds under the little uneasy wind; a flurry of startled voices; footsteps below in the courtyard. Somewhere a woman cried out, "Now God save us!"

She set aside her frame and rose, spilling bright silks from her lap, and looked out of the window. Below in the inner courtyard people were gathering. She saw how they gathered in little knots, speaking together and yet seeming lost and unknowing of what to do with themselves; here and there one glanced up towards her window, and she saw their faces stunned-looking in the fading daylight, and suddenly she was cold afraid.

"Nesta," she said, "do you go down to the inner court and ask if word has come from Benwick. It is in my heart that something is amiss."

And the maiden Nesta went out and down the winding stair.

Scarcely was she gone than the heavy door opened again, and Mordred stood within the opening, Mordred clad in his usual midnight black that he wore as other men wore rose-scarlet, and playing gently with a peacock's feather, so that, meeting his gaze where she stood with the bright tangle of silks at her feet, the Queen felt as though she were being stared at by three bright unwinking eyes instead of two.

"What is it?" she said.

And he answered her with exquisite gentleness, "Letters have come from Benwick. Arthur and Lancelot are both slain."

For a moment the Queen's world swam and darkened, and all she saw clearly were the three eyes gazing at her, bright and mocking. But something in their gaze told her beyond all doubt that he was lying. And the world steadied again.

And she heard her own voice saying, cool and calm, "I do not believe you."

"Other people will," he said, "other people do. Do you not hear them?"

Somewhere in the castle a woman was weeping, and from St Stephen's church a bell began to toll.

"I can show you the letters," Mordred said, smiling pleasantly; and she saw that he was so sure of himself that he did not care whether she believed him or not.

Still, she would not yield. "Anyone can forge such

letters and claim that they came from Benwick," she said. "A few bribes –"

Mordred's smile grew wider as he agreed. "Anyone. Nevertheless, the people will believe. It will be true in a short while, in any case. And meanwhile, I go to make ready for my crowning."

"Your *crowning?*" said the Queen.

"Of course. The High King is dead, Britain must have her new High King."

And the Queen knew that it would serve no purpose to plead, nor to cry out upon him. Neither pleading nor wrath could touch him, for he breathed a higher and colder air than other men, and was beyond the reach of such things. So she said only, "Go now. You have told me what you came to tell, and I would be alone."

But the worst shock was still to come.

"I will go," said Mordred. "But presently I shall come again, from my crowning, and with the High King's circlet on my head, for there is another matter on which I would speak with you."

"There is no other matter on which I have need to speak with you," said the Queen.

"Ah, but there is: for it concerns you nearly. The matter of our marriage."

Then the Queen did indeed cry out on him; a small, desperate cry, "Our *marriage?* Mordred, you are mad!"

Mordred reached out the mocking peacock's feather and touched her cheek, and she jerked her head back as though from the touch of a hot coal. "Nay, I speak good sense. With you to sit beside me, my claim to the High Kingship will be the more sure – and *you*, my sweet lady, will still be the Queen."

"Mordred!" the Queen cried in horror. "I am your father's wife!"

"Widow."

"Widow or wife, it is all one in this matter. I am your stepmother!"

"A fat purse of gold to the Church, and the Church shall cut that tangle swift enough," Mordred said. And then, "Seeing that after all there is no shared blood between us as there was between my father and *my* mother."

And looking into his eyes, the Queen understood for the first time the full depth of his hatred for the High King.

Somehow she wrenched her gaze from his, and made a great show of stooping to gather up her embroidery silks. She knew that she must play for time. "When the High King hears of this, he will come back –" she began.

And Mordred said, "When the High King hears – *if* the High King hears – it will be too late."

"You must give me time," she whispered, "time to think – to pray . . ."

And Mordred said, "Surely I will give you time; all that lies between now and tomorrow's morning. Think and pray as much as you wish, madam; in the end you must yield yourself to do as I will."

And he turned and left the chamber.

The Queen stood where he had left her, alone and unmoving, until in a little while Nesta returned, white-faced, with the grievous news as she had heard it in the inner courtyard. Then the Queen opened her clenched hand; and the brilliant silks for the angels' wings fell to the ground again, stained with blood where she had closed her hand upon the needle hidden within them without ever knowing it.

"It is all lies," she said, "all lies." And she told the maiden of Mordred's visit and what had passed between them; and when Nesta began to shiver and cry out what should they do, she said, "Peace, my maiden; I am thinking what we shall do. I am thinking now!"

She knew that she must get away from Camelot, where she was surrounded by men of Mordred's following. At London, the royal castle was still held by Sir Galagars, an old and faithful knight of the Round Table, who she was sure would still be true to Arthur. If she could get there and put herself under his protection; under the protection also of Dubricius, the aged Archbishop, she might be safe. But before all else, she must get word to Arthur of his son's treachery.

So she bade Nesta to bring her pen, ink and parchment, and set herself to write a letter, bidding the girl meanwhile to find a certain one among her household squires, and bring him to her with all speed, telling him nothing on the way lest they be overheard. She feared that already her own household might have been taken from her and replaced by Mordred's men. But she had not yet finished her desperate letter when her maiden returned, and the squire Hew with her.

The young man knelt at her feet. "Oh, my lady – the King –"

"The King is not dead," she said quickly, still writing. "It is all an evil plot of Mordred's to seize the Crown and force me to wed with him." And while the squire gasped and stammered between astonishment

and relief and fury, she finished the letter, warning
her lord of what was going forward, and telling him
also of what she herself planned to do. Then she folded
it, and sealed the packet with a little engraved stone
that hung among the jewels at her neck.

"Hew," she said, "will you ride for me again, as
you rode for me when Sir Meliagraunce had me
captive in his power?"

"To the world's end, my lady!" said the squire.

"Nay, not so far. But to Benwick. Get out of Camelot
this night and make for the south coast. Take the
first ship you can find. I will give you journey-gold
for the passage; also for a horse – it may be that you
will have to escape from here on foot – and carry this
to the High King with all speed!"

Even as she spoke, giving the packet into his eager
hand, she heard a distant roar of voices from the Great
Hall, and the bright neigh of trumpets, and knew that
Mordred was already proclaiming himself High King.

That night, under cover of the first dark, the squire
got out from Camelot as from an enemy camp, and
headed for the south coast, bearing the Queen's letter.

And in the morning Guenever, who had lain wakeful
all night, bade her maidens to dress her in her finest
blue-violet gown, and painted her eyes and her lips and
put on her finest jewels. And when Mordred came
again to her chamber, she received him sitting stately
in her great cushioned chair beside the hearth. And
she looked on him more kindly than ever she had done
before, even though the golden circlet of the Pendragon was upon his head.

Mordred noticed the blue-violet gown and the

jewels and the kinder aspect, and smiled within himself, thinking that he knew what they meant. "Madam, I had forgotten in the time since Lancelot went overseas how beautiful you are," he said. "You have been thinking of the matter of our marriage that we spoke of last night?"

"I have been thinking," said the Queen. "Yesterday I was startled and angry and spoke in haste; but the more I thought, the more I came to see that since I am in your power and you can force me to do what you will, it would be but foolishness to struggle against you. Therefore" – she smiled ruefully, speaking to him as though half in jest, in the words of a knight beaten in the joust to the victor who stands over him with a drawn sword – "I yield me, and cry your mercy . . . If Archbishop Dubricius gives us the Church's leave, I will marry you – and as you yourself said, I shall still be the Queen."

"Madam, you are wise as well as beautiful!" said Sir Mordred. "I will send word to the Archbishop within this hour. And a gift of gold."

The Queen shook her head. "Sending word will not be enough. Nor will a gift of gold. I must speak with him myself."

"As you will," said Mordred. "I will have him sent for."

"Nay," said the Queen, "he is very old: too old to travel lightly, and of too high estate to be whistled for like a dog. If we are to gain his leave, I must go to him as a suppliant –" And then, as she saw refusal in his face, "Give me until tomorrow's morning to make ready for the journey; and if you fear that I plan some escape, send a strong escort of your own knights

with me, so that you allow me also to have certain of
my own maidens for my company. Indeed you have
no more choice than I; for if I come to the Archbishop
in supplication, and show myself willing for this marriage, it is in my mind that I shall win from him the
Church's leave. Then I will marry you, as I have said;
but without the Church's leave I cannot be your wife;
and indeed our marriage would weaken, not strengthen,
your claim to the High Kingship."

So Sir Mordred yielded to the Queen's demands; and
next morning, with her favourite maidens about her,
and a strong escort of Sir Mordred's men, she set out
for London.

Five days they were upon the journey, lodging in
royal manors or in abbey guest-houses along the way.
For the heavy ox-drawn cart with its cushions and
tented tapestry hangings made slow travelling along
the rutted roads that were still more like watercourses
after the winter rains. And every lurching, jolting
wheel-turn of the way, the Queen's heart was out
before her, straining towards the grey-walled castle
that was her only hope of safety from the terrible fair-
haired man behind her, and where she and Sir Galagars
might make a strong point to hold for the rightful
king. And always she wondered how it was with her
young squire; how far he had got on the way to Benwick;
if he was on the way to Benwick at all, or lying dead
in a ditch somewhere, and her letter already in Mordred's hands.

When they reached London at last, she found that
they were not to lodge in the King's castle as she had
always done, but in the royal manor, just outside the
city. Her maidens looked at her with anxious eyes; but

after she had had a little time to think, it seemed to the Queen that this was a difficulty easily overcome, and without the fighting in the outer courtyard that must have followed had she ridden in through the castle gates to claim Sir Galagars's protection with a score of Mordred's men around her. She had been beyond caring that she was leading her escort into a trap, but the life of every man still loyal to her lord the King was precious to her, and some of them also would have died in the fighting.

The next day very early in the morning, the Queen bade horses to be brought round; for she and her maidens would go to pray at a certain shrine and holy well to Our Lady in the fields near Westminster, where she sometimes went when the King held his court in London. All her life, save in the fighting times, she had been used to ride abroad whenever she would, with no escort save a few of her ladies with her. And the knights of Sir Mordred's following had no good reason to say her nay, especially with the steward and the manor people all around to hear. So the palfreys were brought round; and muffled close in thick-furred mantles against the chill March wind that blew upriver, the Queen and her maidens set out towards Our Lady's shrine.

But as soon as they were beyond sight of the manor, they changed direction, turning into a narrow lane that led towards London and, setting their palfreys to a swifter pace, rode hard for the city and the royal stronghold, through the wind and the scurrying spring rain.

And so a while later those within the castle heard a great beating upon the main gate, and when it was opened, in rode a little company of wet and storm-blown women. And as the foremost of them flung back her hood, the men of the gate-guard knew her for the Queen.

"Make the gates fast!" she cried to them. "Enemies of my Lord the King will be here before long!"

They made haste to do her bidding, while pages and squires came to aid her and her maidens to dismount, and hard behind them Sir Galagars came swiftly to receive her. And when he heard what she had to tell, he was greatly wrath, and the castle was made secure to withstand all that Sir Mordred, now calling himself the High King, might bring against it.

And when the escort found how the Queen had escaped from them, they sent hurried word to Mordred, the usurper, and he gathered all the fighting men who were of his following and near at hand and sent out his summons to those who were further off to gather to him in London. And in a frenzy at seeing his smooth plans beginning to go awry, he rode for London with all speed, leaving the foot soldiers to follow after. And when he reached London, he sat down all about the castle to lay siege to it.

And he sent in heralds under the green branch with rich gifts for the Queen, bidding her leave this foolishness and come out to her wedding.

But the Queen sent back his gifts, the jewels and the rare perfumes and the pair of milk-white hounds, and with them her message, short and to the point, "Nay, I come not out from these walls, false traitor, for rather than wed with you, I will die by my own hand!"

Then came Dubricius the Archbishop, small and wizened with age, but with eyes like hot coals in his sunken face, and he entered Mordred's camp, his clergy about him, and cried out upon the usurper, "Sir, what will you do? Will you first anger God and then shame yourself and all knighthood? The Queen is your father's wife, and how may you wed with her without mortal sin?"

"My father is dead," said Mordred, biting the words off one by one.

"Even if that were true, still would she be your stepmother; still would a marriage between you be mortal sin!"

"*My father is dead*," repeated Mordred. "And I am the new High King, with the High King's powers. Therefore cease your prating, for I will silence you by having your head struck from your shoulders, if there is no other way!"

"I do not believe that Arthur is slain," said the old man. "And I am not the only man in Britain to believe that this tale of his death is but a foul lie set about by yourself that you may seize his power in the land, and his Queen with all! I too can threaten, and I bid you to leave off from this evil, or I will curse you with bell and with book and with candle!"

"Curse and be cursed to you!" cried Mordred, and his silken smile had become a snarl; but he dared make no attempt against the old man, for there was a cold doubt in his heart whether even his own men would obey him if he ordered them to seize the Archbishop.

So the Archbishop withdrew to the great abbey church, and gathered the monks under their abbot and his own clergy about him. And there before the high altar where he had set the High King's circlet upon Arthur's head more than thirty years ago, he cursed Arthur's son by bell and by book and by candle, cutting him off from all the rights and blessings of the Christian Church.

With all the forms and ceremonies of the Church, and with all the strength that was within himself, he cursed him; and when the cursing was finished, he was empty and spent, and knew that he was old; old beyond his Archbishophood, and the last of his strength for the battles of good and evil upon this earth was gone from him.

Then he thought of Merlin, who had stood with him on the day that Arthur was crowned: Merlin with his own strength spent, since then, long ago gone to his enchanted sleep. Not for him, Dubricius, that long quiet darkness under the magic hawthorn tree; but in his last years the quiet of loneliness and poverty and prayer. So he took his leave of those about him, and wearing the rusty habit of a poor monk, and mounted on a mule, he rode out from London city, none guessing as the threadbare and hooded figure passed them by that the great Archbishop rode that way.

And so he went, day by day, until he came to Avalon of the Apple Trees. And there he found the little wattle-built abbey church and its beehive cells surrounding it, that Joseph of Arimathea and his companions had built when first he came to Britain carrying the Holy Grail. Through all the years between, men had dwelt there, living a life of prayer and of help to the poor. But slowly their numbers had dwindled. The living-huts were empty now, and freshly turned earth lay over the grave of the last of the brotherhood.

And in London, Mordred sent again to the Queen, with gifts and fair speeches, begging her to come out to him; but she sent back the same answer as before, that she would die by her own hand before she became his wife. And then in wrath and growing fear, he set to lay siege to the castle in good earnest; and every day his war-host grew, as more and more of his following from up and down the land came in answer to his summons.

But still the royal castle held against them, and they could not come at the Queen.

And meanwhile, the squire Hew had reached Arthur's camp before Benwick Castle, and brought the Queen's letter to the King's pavilion, where he sat late with Sir Gawain, whom he had summoned to share a cup of wine with him in the hope that he might yet be able to persuade him not to ride out again next morning against Sir Lancelot.

He took the letter from the mired and weary squire, and broke the seal, and read it through without a word. And without a word he gave it to Sir Gawain.

And while Sir Gawain read it also, there was silence within the tent; a core of silence amid the sounds of the camp and the bluster of the spring gale blowing outside. But when he reached the end of the letter, Gawain let out a great roar, baffled and grief-stricken like some wild thing in a trap, and flung the closely written parchment on the bed-place beside him and buried his battered head in his arms.

The King picked up the letter again, and gentled it in his hand because the Queen had written it and found means to send it to him, while at the same time grief and anger at the news it brought tore each other within him. And he sent his tent squires to beg this one and that among his war-leaders to come to him; and then began to ask the squire Hew for more details than were in the letter. And while he was doing so, Sir Gawain lurched to his feet and caught up his sword-belt that he had slackened off and laid beside him earlier, and began to buckle it on again, with furious haste, as though the enemy were in the windy dark outside the tent-flap.

And the King looked at him and said, "Sir Gawain, you are excused this warfare."

But Sir Gawain raised bloodshot eyes to his face, and said, "Sir, of all the warfares and quarrels of my life, this is the one that I would least hold back from."

"It will be to fight your own brother; your last remaining brother."

"I have no brothers now!" Gawain roared. "Mordred is more dead to me than all the rest. I am all that is left of the Orkney brood, and I am your man as I always have been."

So next day the King's camp was struck, and the war-host marched away towards the coast, Sir Gawain with the rest of them. And watching from the ramparts of Benwick Castle, with a puzzled frown between his brows, Sir Bors said to Sir Lancelot beside him, "Now what could draw them away so suddenly – unless it be ill news from Britain?"

"Ill news or not," said Sir Lancelot, "it can be no matter that concerns us any more." But his eyes followed the last moving flicker of the distant rear-guard until it disappeared into the forest, and he would

have given all that he had in life if it could have been
his concern again.

The King and his army came to the coast, and when
the hastily summoned fleet had gathered, they took
ship again for Britain. But Mordred had got word of
their coming; and when, after a stormy crossing, they
drew at last to land at Dover, they found the usurper
and all his rebel war-host waiting for them.

Then the King's trumpets and the rebel trumpets
crowed against each other in the wild spring dawn;
and there began a great and terrible struggle that
lasted all day, as the King's men ran their ships ashore
and sprang overboard into the shallows, and the rebels
came charging out to meet them. A battle fought out
in the grey swinging shallows of the Narrow Seas,
and on the sloping shingle that was soon running red,
and along the cliff paths and among the chalky
hummocks and the coarse wind-shivered grass. Until
at evening the cold spitting rain died out, and the
skies broke up and let through a sodden yellow gleam
and the King's men gained the cliff-tops and swept
them clear, as Mordred and his men gave back and
broke, and streamed away into the eye of the wild
sunset.

But the victory had been sorely paid for, and the
bodies of knights and men-at-arms lay dark like sea-
wrack along the tide-line and up the cliff paths and
clotted thick about the stranded ships. And the King,
having given orders for the succouring of his wounded
and the burying of his dead, knelt beside Sir Gawain
in the small rough chamber high in Dover Castle
where he had been carried by the men who had found

him lying among the dead with the old wound in his head burst open again by a fresh blow.

Gawain opened his eyes and looked at him by the light of the kelp fire burning on the hearth. "I am for death, this time," he said.

And bending over the narrow cot, Arthur put his arms round him and raised him a little, and said, "Ah Gawain, Gawain, my most dear nephew, you and Lancelot I loved best of all my knights; and now I have lost you both, and all my earthly joy is gone."

"And it is all my doing," said Sir Gawain, stumbling over the words with a tongue that seemed made of wood. "For if Sir Lancelot had been with you as once he was, this grievous war would never have come about . . . And now you have need of Lancelot more than ever you had before, and it is through my hunger for revenge that you have lost him, when he had no ill-will towards either you or me . . . And I – I would be at peace with him now, but it is too late." And lying against the King's shoulder, he closed his eyes so that it seemed as though he swooned or slept. But when the King would have laid him down, he opened them again and asked, "Is there pen and parchment to be found in this castle?"

"Lie still, and never trouble for pen and parchment now," said the King.

"It is the last thing that I shall do in the world," mumbled Sir Gawain. "But I must write to Sir Lancelot, who was once my friend . . ."

And when pen and parchment and a taper were brought to him by one of the clerks who moved always with the war-host, he wrote with great difficulty, the King propping and steadying him the while.

"Unto Sir Lancelot, flower of all noble knights that ever I saw or heard of, I, Gawain, send you greetings, and beg your forgiveness in the name of the old friendship that was between us. In the name of that same friendship, come with all speed and with every knight and fighting-man that you can muster, for the traitor Mordred has raised rebellion against our Lord the King, who is in sore need of your sword. Mordred has made the people to believe him slain, and sought to take the Queen for his wife, who has shut herself away from him in the royal castle in London. This day we landed at Dover and put the traitor to flight, but there must be much more fighting ere all be done. In this day's battle I received a sore dunt upon my head, in the very place where you wounded me before Benwick Castle, and I write this to you in the hour of my death. Come swiftly, before Mordred can gather more rebel troops. Pray for my soul when you come beside my grave; but Arthur lives and has great need of you, and without your coming the Kingdom of Logres is lost. I write to you as with my heart's blood. Farewell."

Towards the end of the letter the writing began to wander and stray across the page; and when the last word was written, the quill dropped from Sir Gawain's hand, and his head fell back. "Pray you send this," he said.

"I will send it," the King promised, and kissed him on his battered forehead. His eyes closed, and when the King laid him down this time he did not open them again.

7

THE LAST BATTLE

Mordred had fled away westward, and as he went, he harried the lands of those who would not join him. But there were many, in the days that followed, who did join him; for fear because the thing had gone too far for them to expect mercy from Arthur now, or because they chose the usurper's lawless rule, or simply because they had loved Lancelot, and for his sake would draw sword for any leader who was against Arthur, which was the saddest reason of all. Yet there were as many who took up their arms and came in to

fight for their rightful king; and so when the High
King also hurried westward in pursuit of his traitor
son, there was little to choose for size and strength
between the two war-hosts.

They swept past London, along the great ridge
that reared its back above the forest country; and the
King longed to check and ride for the city for one
last sight of Guenever the Queen. But it was not the
time, and he contented himself as best he might by
sending three messengers on fast horses to make
enquiry and bring him back word that all was well
with her, while he pushed on westward without slack-
ening the pace and purpose of his march.

Twice the war-hosts met in battle, and twice the
High King thrust the usurper back. And so at last, far
over into the western marsh-country, the two armies
faced each other for the greatest battle of all, encamped
upon opposite sides of a level plain bleak and open
among the wet woods in their first springtime green
and the winding waterways of those parts. And when
Arthur asked of an old woman who came in to sell
eggs and cheese in the royal camp, "Old mother, is
there a name to this place?" she said, "Aye, this is the
plain of Camlann."

That night, when all things had been made ready
for the battle that must come next day, Arthur lay in
his pavilion and could not sleep. Beyond the looped-
back entrance where his squires lay, the open plain
stretched away like a dark sea, with the hushing of
the wind through the long grass and the furze scrub
for the sounding of the waves, to where the enemy
watch-fires marked its further shore. His mind seemed
full of whirling memories, and the sea-sound sank and

changed into the whisper of reeds round the margin of still water . . . Still water . . . Lake water lapping . . . And Merlin standing beside him on the day that he received Excalibur. Merlin's voice in his ears again across all the years between, saying, "Over there is Camlann, the place of the Last Battle . . . But that is another story; and for another day as yet far off."

Now the day was here, waiting beyond the darkness of this one spring night. A night that was dark indeed. The doom that he had unwittingly loosed so long ago when all unknowing, he fathered Mordred upon his own half-sister, was upon him, and upon all that he had fought for. And tomorrow he and Mordred must be the death of each other. And what of Britain after that? Torn in two, and with the Sea Wolves and the men of the North waiting to come swarming in again?

In the chill dark hour before dawn, he fell into a state between sleeping and waking. And in that state he dreamed a dream – if it was a dream.

It seemed to him that Sir Gawain came in through the entrance to the tent, armed and looking just as he used to, though it was maybe strange that he came pacing in as though no tent squires lay across the threshold, and none of them seemed to see him come. And Arthur sat up and stretched his arms to him in joyful greeting. "Welcome! Gawain, my most dear nephew! Now thanks be to God that I see you hale and living, for I thought you dead and grave-laid in Dover town!" And then he saw that behind Gawain thronged the bright-eyed misty shapes of women, foremost among them the Lady Ragnell, Gawain's seven-years' wife; and he was glad that Gawain had found his own lady again, for the years that he had shared with her had been his best as a knight and as a man. And Arthur asked, "But what of these ladies who come with you?"

"Sir," said Gawain, "these be all of them ladies whom I fought for or served in some way when I was man alive. God has listened to their prayers and for their sakes has been merciful to me and granted that I come to you."

"It is for some urgent cause that you come," said the King.

"It is to forewarn you of your death. For if you join battle with Sir Mordred this day, as you and he are both set to do, you must both die, and the greater part of your followings with you, and the Kingdom of Logres shall indeed go down into the dark. Therefore God, of his special grace, has sent me to bid you not to fight this day, but to find means to make a treaty with Sir Mordred, promising whatever he asks of you as the price of this delay. A truce that shall gain you one month of time; for within that month shall come Sir Lancelot and all his following, and together you shall overcome Sir Mordred and his war-host, and so shall the kingdom be saved from the dark."

And suddenly, with his last word scarcely spoken, he was gone from the place where he had been and the bright-eyed shadows with him.

And in a little, Arthur saw the green light of dawn growing pale beyond the tent flaps. Then he arose and summoned his squires to fetch Sir Lucan and Sir Bedivere and two of his churchmen. And when they came and stood before him, he told them of the vision he had had, and the thing that Sir Gawain had told him. And he charged them to go to Sir Mordred under the green branch, and make truce with him that should last a month. "Offer him lands and goods," said the King, "as much as seem reasonable – anything that seems reasonable. Only do you win for me and for all our people this month's delay."

So Sir Bedivere and Sir Lucan and the two church-men went forth under the green branch, and came to the enemy camp. And there they spoke long with Sir Mordred among his grim war-host of fifty thousand men. And at last Mordred agreed to these terms: that he should have the lands of Kent and the old Kingdom of Cornwall from that day forward, and the whole of Britain after the King's death.

It was agreed between them that Arthur and Mordred should meet an hour from noon, midway between the two war-camps, and each accompanied by only fourteen knights and their squires, for the signing of the treaty.

And Sir Bedivere and Sir Lucan returned to the royal camp and told Arthur what had been arranged; and when he heard them, a great relief arose in him, for he thought that maybe after all God was showing him a way to turn back the dark and to save Britain. But still, he did not trust his son, and he had the men of his war-host drawn up clear of the camp and facing the enemy, and when the horses were brought, and he mounted, his chosen fourteen knights around him, and he was ready to ride out to the meeting, he said to the captains, "If you see any sword drawn, wait for no orders, but come on fiercely, and slay all that you may, for there is a black shadow on my heart, and I do not trust Sir Mordred."

And on the other side of the plain, Mordred gave

orders to his own war-host: "If you see any sword drawn, come on with all speed and slay all that stand against you, for I do not trust this treaty, and I know well that my father will seek to be revenged on me."

And so they rode forward, and met at the appointed place midway between the battle-hosts, and dismounted, leaving their horses in the care of their squires, to discuss and sign the treaty, which the clerks had made out twice over upon fine sheets of vellum. Then the treaty was agreed, and first Arthur and then Mordred signed it, using the King's saddle for a writing slope; and when that was done, wine was brought and first Arthur and then Mordred drank together, both from the same cup. And it seemed that there must be peace between them, at least for this one month, and the doom and the darkness turned aside.

But scarcely had they drunk and their copies of the treaty been fairly exchanged, when an adder, rousing in the warmth of the spring day, and disturbed by the trampling of men and horses too near her sleeping place, slithered out from among the dry grass roots, coil upon liquid coil, and bit one of Mordred's knights through some loose lacing of the chain-mail at his heel.

And when the knight felt the fiery smart, he looked down and saw the adder, and unthinkingly he drew his sword and slashed the small wicked thing in half.

And when both war-hosts saw the stormy sunlight flash on the naked blade, they remembered their orders, and the harm was done. From both sides there rose a great shouting and a blowing of horns and trumpets, and the two war-hosts burst forward and rolled towards each other, dark as doom under their coloured standards and fluttering pennants, jinking with points of light like the flicker of summer lightning in the heart of a thunder-cloud, where the sour yellow sunshine struck on sword-blade and spear-point; and giving out a swelling storm roar of hooves and war cries and weapon-jar as they came.

Then Arthur cried out in a terrible voice, "Alas! This most accursed day!" And hurling himself into the saddle, drove spurs into his horse's flanks, and swung him round with frantic haste to join the fore-front of his own on-coming war-host. Sir Mordred did likewise in the same instant; and the battle closed around them both.

The sorest and most savage battle that ever was fought in any land of Christendom.

It was scarcely past noon when the fighting joined, but soon the clouds that gathered overhead made it seem like evening; and as the dark battle masses swept and swirled this way and that, lit by blade-flash and torn by the screams of smitten horses and the war-shouts and the death-cries of men, so the black cloud mass that arched above them seemed to boil as though at the heart of some mighty tempest, echoing the spear tempest upon Camlann Plain beneath. And many a terrible blow was given and many mighty champions fell; and old enemies fought each other in the reeling press, and friend fought friend and brother fought brother. And as the time went by the ranks of both war-hosts grew thinner, and more and more the feet of the living were clogged by the bodies of the dead; and one by one the banners and pennants that were tattered as the ragged sky went down into the mire; and all the mire of Camlann's trampled plain oozed red.

And all day long Mordred and the High King rode through the thick of the battle and came by no hurt, so that it seemed as though they held charmed lives; and ever in the reeling thick of the fighting they sought for each other, but might never come together all the black day long.

And so day drew to the edge of night; and a great and terrible stillness settled over the plain; and Arthur, who had had three horses killed under him since noon, stood to draw breath and look about him. And all was red; the blade of his own sword crimsoned to the hilt, and the sodden mire into which the grass was trampled down; even the underbellies of the clouds that had been dark all day were stained red by the light of the setting sun. And nothing moved over all Camlann Plain but the ravens circling black-winged against that smouldering sky; and nothing sounded save the howl of a wolf far off, and near at hand the cry of a dying man.

And Arthur saw that two men stood close behind him; and one was old Sir Lucan and the other Sir Bedivere, and both sore wounded. And of all the men who had followed him back from Benwick or gathered to his standard on the march from Dover, and of all those men, also, who had been his before they were drawn from their loyalty by Mordred's treachery or by their love for Lancelot, these two, leaning wearily on their swords beside him, were all who remained alive.

And the black bitterness of death rose in Arthur the King, and a mighty groan burst from him.

"Grief of God! That I should see this day! Grief upon me for all my noble knights that lie here slain! Now indeed I know that the end is come. But before all things go down into the dark – where is Sir Mordred who has brought about this desolation?"

Then as he looked about him, he became aware of one more figure still upon its feet; Sir Mordred in hacked and battered armour, standing at a little distance, alone in the midst of a sprawling tangle of dead men.

And Arthur would not use Excalibur upon his own son; and so, to Sir Lucan who stood nearest to him, he said, "Give me a spear; for yonder stands the man who brought this day into being, and the thing is not yet ended between us two."

"Sir, let him be!" said Sir Lucan. "He is accursed! And if you let this day of ill destiny go by, you shall be most fully avenged upon him at another time. My liege lord, pray you remember your last night's dream, and what the spirit of Gawain told you. Even though by God's grace and mercy you still live at the day's end, yet leave off the fighting now; for there are three of us, while Sir Mordred stands alone, and therefore we have won the field; and once the doom day be passed, it will be passed indeed, and new days to come."

But, "Give me life or give me death," said Arthur, "the thing is not finished until I have slain my son who has brought destruction upon Logres and upon all Britain, and for whom so many good men lie slain."

"Then God speed you well," said Sir Bedivere.

And Sir Lucan gave the King his spear, and he grasped it in both hands and made at a stumbling run for the solitary figure. The terrible red drunkenness of battle was upon him, and he cried out as he ran, "Traitor! Now is your death-time upon you!"

And hearing him, Sir Mordred lifted his head, and recognised death, and with drawn sword came to meet him. And so they ran, stumbling over the dead, and came together in the midst of that dreadful reddened field, under that dreadful bleeding sky. And the High King smote his son under the shield with a great thrust of his spear, that pierced him clean through the body. And when Sir Mordred felt his death wound within him, he gave a great yell, savage and despairing, and thrust himself forward upon the spear-shaft, as a boar carried forward by its own rush up the shaft of the hunter, until he was stayed by the hand-guard; and with all the last of his strength he swung up his sword two-handed, and dealt the High King his father such a blow on the side of the dragon-crested helmet that the blade sliced through helm and mail-coif and deep into the skull beneath. And at the end of the blow Sir Mordred fell stark dead upon the spear, dragging it with him to the ground. And in the same instant Arthur the King dropped also, not dead but in a black swoon, upon the stained and trampled earth.

Then Sir Lucan and Sir Bedivere came and lifted him between them, and by slow stages, for their wounds were sore upon them, they bore him from the battle-field, and to a little ruined chapel not far off, and laid him there in the shelter and quiet that the place offered, upon a bed of piled fern that looked as though it had been made ready for him, before the altar.

And there, when they laid him down, Sir Lucan gave a deep groan and crumpled to the earth at his feet; for the effort of getting his king to shelter had been too great for him, with the gaping wound that was in his belly.

And when Arthur, coming back to himself, saw Sir Lucan's body sprawled there, the grief rose in him, and he cried out "Alas, this is a sore sight! He would have aided me, and he had more need of aid himself!"

And Sir Bedivere knelt weeping beside the dead knight, for they had loved each other as brothers since the days when the Round Table was young.

It had been dark when they reached the chapel, but now the skies had cleared, and presently the moon arose, sailing high and uncaring above the dreadful stillness of Camlann Plain. And looking with shadowed sight out through the gap in the far wall where the stones had fallen, Arthur saw not far off the whispering reed-fringed shores of a lake. White mists scarfed the water, shimmering in the white fire of the moon; and the far shores were lost in mist and moonshine, so that there might have been no far shore at all. And Arthur knew that lake. He knew it to his heart's core.

And gathering all that was left of his strength, he said to Sir Bedivere, "To this lake . . . To another part of this lake, Merlin brought me, long ago . . ." And it seemed to him that he was forcing the words out so hard that they must come forth as a shout, but they came only as a ragged whisper that Sir Bedivere must bend close to hear. "Now leave your weeping; there will be time for mourning later on for you – but for me, my time with you grows short, and there is yet one thing more that I must have you do for me."

"Anything," said Sir Bedivere, "anything, my liege lord . . ."

"Take you Excalibur, my good sword, and carry it down to yonder lakeshore, and throw it far out into the water. Then come again and tell me what you see."

"My lord," said Bedivere, "I will do as you command, and bring you word."

And he took the great sword from where it lay beside the King and, reeling with weakness from his own wounds, made his way down to the water's brink.

In that place, alder trees grew here and there along the bank, and he passed through them, stooping under the low branches, and paused, looking down at the great sword in his hands; and the white fire of the moon showed him the jewels in the hilt and played like running water between the clotted stains on the faery-forged blade. And he thought, "This is not only a High King's weapon, this is the sword of Arthur, and once thrown into the lake it will be lost for ever, and an ill thing that would be."

And the more he looked, the more he weakened in his purpose. And at last he turned from the water and hid Excalibur among the roots of the alder trees.

Then he went back to Arthur.

"Have you done as I bade you?" said Arthur.

"Sir, it is done," said Bevidere.

"And what did you see?"

"Sir," said Bedivere, "what should I see under the moon, but the bright ripples spreading in the waters of the lake?"

"That is not truly spoken," said the King, "therefore go back to the lake, and as you are dear to me, carry out my command."

So Sir Bedivere went back to the lakeshore, and

took the sword from its hiding place, fully meaning this time to do as the King had bidden him. But again the white fire of the moon blazed upon the jewelled hilt and the sheeny blade, and he felt the power of it in his hands as though it had been a live thing. And he thought, "If ever men gather again to thrust back the dark, as we thrust it back when the Table and the world were young, this is the only true sword for whoever leads them." And he returned the sword to its hiding place, and went back to the chapel where the King lay waiting for him.

"Have you done my bidding, this second time?" asked the King.

"I cast Excalibur far out into the lake," said Sir Bedivere.

"And what did you see?"

"Only the reeds stirring in the night wind."

And the King said in a harsh and anguished whisper, "I had thought Mordred the only traitor among the brotherhood; but now you have betrayed me twice. I have loved you; counted you among the noblest of my knights of the Round Table, and you would break faith with me for the richness of a sword."

Bedivere knelt beside him with hanging head. "Not for the richness, my liege lord," he said at last. "I am ashamed; but it was not for the richness, not for the jewels in the hilt nor the temper of the blade."

"That I know," the King said, more gently. "Yet now, go again swiftly; and this time do not fail me, if you value still my love."

And Sir Bedivere got stiffly to his feet, and went a third time down to the water's edge, and took the great sword from its hiding place; and a third time he felt the power of it in his hand and saw the white moon-fire on the blade; but without pause he swung it up above his head, and flung it with the last strength of arm and breast and shoulder, far out into the lake.

He waited for the splash, but there was none, for out of the misty surface of the lake rose a hand and arm clad in white samite, that met and caught it by the hilt. Three times it flourished Excalibur in slow wide circles of farewell, and then vanished back into the water, taking the great sword with it from the eyes of this world. And no widening ring of ripples told where it was gone.

Sir Bedivere, blind with tears, turned and stumbled back to the chapel and his waiting lord.

"It is done as you commanded," he said.

"And what did you see?" said the King.

"I saw a hand that came out of the lake, and an arm clothed in white samite; and the hand caught Excalibur and brandished it three times as though in leave-taking – and so withdrew, bearing the sword with it, beneath the water."

"That was truly spoken and well done," said the King; and he raised himself on his elbow. "Now I must go hence. Aid me down to the water side."

And Sir Bedivere aided him to his feet and took his weight upon his own shoulder, and half-supported, half-carried him down to the lakeshore.

And there, where before had seemed to be only the lapping water and the reeds whispering in the moon-light, a narrow barge draped all in black lay as though it waited for them, within the shadows of the alder trees. And in it were three ladies, black-robed, and their hair veiled in black beneath the queenly crowns they wore. And their faces alone, and their outstretched hands, showed white as they sat looking up at the two on the bank and weeping. And one of them was the Queen of Northgalis, and one was Nimue, the Lady of all the Ladies of the Lake; and the third was Queen Morgan La Fay, freed at last from her own evil now that the dark fate-pattern was woven to its end.

"Now lay me in the barge, for it has been waiting for me long," said Arthur, and Sir Bedivere aided him down the bank, and gently lowered him to the hands of the three black-robed queens, who made soft mourning as they received him and laid him down. And the Lady of the Lake took his battered head into her lap; and kneeling beside him, Queen Morgan la Fay said, "Alas, dear brother, you have tarried overlong from us and your wound has grown chilled."

And the barge drifted out from the shadows under the alder trees, leaving Sir Bedivere standing alone upon the bank.

And Sir Bedivere cried out like a child left in the dark, "Oh, my Lord Arthur, what shall become of me, now that you go hence and leave me here alone?"

And the King opened his eyes and looked at him for the last time. "Comfort yourself, and do the best that you may, for I must be gone into the Vale of Avalon, for the healing of my grievous wound. One day I will return, in time of Britain's sorest need, but not even I know when that day may be, save that it is afar off . . . But if you hear no more of me in the world of men, pray for my soul."

And the barge drifted on, into the white mist between the water and the moon. And the mist received it, and it was gone. Only for a little, Sir Bedivere, straining after it, seemed to catch a low desolate wailing as of women keening for their dead.

And then that too was gone, and only the reeds whispered on the desolate lakeshore.

And Sir Bedivere turned and stumbled away, making for the dark woodshore that was not far off and seemed to offer shelter from the terrible white moonlight and the loneliness that the barge had left behind.

All night long, blind with grief and stumbling with the weakness of his wounds, he wandered among alder woods and sour willow scrub, until at dawn he came upon a wattle-built chapel with the ruins of living-cells clustered about it. From one cell, less ruined than the rest, came the faint gleam of a rushlight, and sounds of movement within; and making towards it, he fell across the threshold; and the ancient and ragged hermit, who had once been the Archbishop Dubricius, took him in and cared for him.

8

AVALON
OF THE APPLE TREES

As soon as he received Sir Gawain's letter, Sir Lancelot
set to gathering all the fighting men of Benwick, and
when they were gathered, and arms and stores made
ready with all haste, and the needful ships and galleys
brought together, he sailed with them across the
Narrow Seas, and landed in Dover.

From the Dover men he demanded what was the
news of the High King. And they told him of the
battle that had been fought out there on the shore,

close on a month before, and how the High King had beaten Mordred back and come at last to land; and they told how Sir Mordred had fled away westward with Arthur close upon his heels; and they told him of the shadowy tidings that had come back to them of a last terrible battle fought somewhere in the West, and how in that battle both armies were brought to naught, and Sir Mordred slain, and the King slain also, or, as some said, not slain but borne away into Avalon to be healed of his wounds. But of that, no man knew for sure, and all seemed wrapped in mist and shadows.

But when Sir Lancelot asked as to the fate of Sir Gawain, that they knew full well; and they led him within the castle, to the chapel, and showed him before the altar the new-laid slab of grey stone beneath which the last of the Orkney breed lay buried.

And Sir Lancelot kneeled down, smelling the sea wind through the high unglazed windows, and hearing the crying of the gulls, and wondered if Sir Gawain was in any way aware of them too; and if they seemed to him one with the sea wind and the gulls of his northern home. And there he remained all night, his great ugly head bowed and the tears falling on his joined hands, praying for the soul of Sir Gawain, and weeping for the wild, fiery-haired and fiery-hearted knight who had been for so many years his friend, and then his enemy, and who he now felt to be his friend again.

And in the morning he called all his knights and nobles together and said to them, "My brothers, I thank you all for coming with me into this country, but it seems we come too late; and for that, the grief will be upon me through every day of my life that yet remains to me. Nevertheless, do you wait here under the command of my cousin Sir Bors for one month, and obey and follow him as you would me. But if at the end of that month I have neither returned to you nor sent you any word, then do you return to your own land, and God's grace go with you."

"And you?" said Sir Bors. "What is it that you do, during this month?"

"I go westward," said Sir Lancelot, "first to London, that I may be sure that all is well with the Queen, and thence westward still, towards Avalon; and after that – I do not know."

"Sir," said Sir Bors, "to ride alone through Britain in the present state of the realm is surely madness; for you shall find few enough friends in the wilderness, and may have sore need of trusted men at your back."

"I have ridden the length and breadth of this land with no man at my back before now," said Sir Lancelot, "and found few friends indeed. One man alone may pass easier than a score, if enemies are around; and be that as it may, this is a quest on which I must ride alone. So fare you well."

And next day at the first paling of the morning, he rode away over the downs and through the Wealden forest towards London.

But when he reached London city and came to the royal castle, Sir Galagars the castellan told him that Queen Guenever was no longer there. For close on a month ago word had come to them from Sir Bedivere of the great battle in the West, and of Arthur's passing; and in the night after the word came, she disappeared, and five of her maidens with her.

"Pray you tell me if there is any thought in your mind as to where she can have gone," said Sir Lancelot, swaying with weariness and caked with the mire of hard riding, and fighting down the desire to howl like a dog and strike out at the troubled old knight before him.

And Sir Galagars shook his head and said, "Maybe she has gone westward, towards Avalon."

"And none has sought her?"

"She left word that she knew the place she went to, and none were to seek her," said the old castellan. "And she is still the Queen, her orders to be obeyed. Nevertheless, we have sought her, and found no sign."

Sir Lancelot spent one night in London, and next morning he heard Mass, and then, with a fresh horse under him, set out once more. But now, before all else, he rode westward to find the Queen.

Hither and yon he rode the forest ways while their green flame of springtime darkened towards summer, praying in his heart that he might find her before she came to any harm, and passing often through stretches of burned woodland made hideous by wrecked homesteads and the bones of men and cattle picked bare by gore-crows that marked the path of Mordred's westward march. And wherever he came upon living man or woman, he asked for news of a lady riding with five maidens, who might have passed that way. But no one had seen them go by.

And at last, on the evening of the fifteenth day after leaving London, he came to Almesbury and sought shelter for the night in the great nunnery there. For in those days it was the custom that abbeys both of monks and nuns would have guest-houses within their gates, giving shelter and welcome to all comers, both men and women, be they queens or nobles on fine horses or poor folk who travelled on foot.

So the Lady Abbess made Sir Lancelot welcome, and sent for servants to stable and tend his weary horse, and herself led him towards the guest-chambers.

And as they passed along the cloister, Sir Lancelot saw a nun coming towards them, calm and remote in her habit of black and white. Her head was bent, and he could not see her face in the shadow of her veil. But as they drew nearer to each other, she gave a small breathless cry, and her hands that had been hidden in her wide sleeves flew up to her breast. He would have known her hands anywhere. And she swayed, and crumpled to the ground in a swoon. And Sir Lancelot found himself looking down into the face of Queen Guenever.

He would have stooped to lift her, but the Lady Abbess stayed him with a gesture of one hand, whose calm authority he knew he must not disobey. And other black-and-white sisters came like a gentle flock of birds, and gathered her up and supported her away.

Next morning early, by special consent of the Abbess, Sir Lancelot and the Lady Guenever spoke together in the north cloister walk. It was a most fair morning of early summer, and in the topmost branch of the medlar tree in the midst of the green and peaceful cloister garth a whitethroat was singing. Lancelot gazed long into the face of Guenever who had once been the Queen; and her black hair with the silver strands in it was hidden by her veil, but her eyes were the same willow-grey eyes that he had always known, only that the shadows in them were deeper now.

"So you are come back from Benwick," she said at last. "Was that to help Arthur?"

He bowed his head. "Gawain wrote to me – in the hour of his death – and told me of all that had passed, and the fight at Dover; and that Mordred was fled away westwards and Arthur after him. He told me how that you had taken refuge from Mordred in the royal castle at London. He bade me come, for our liege lord the King had sore need of me. And I gathered my fighting men and came with all speed. But when I reached Dover, the last battle was fought and over, and I was too late. And when I came to London, seeking to know if all was well with you before I went on westward after the King, they told me of Sir Bedivere's message, and how on the night after its coming, you slipped away, and five of your ladies with you, and they could come by no word of you since."

"And so you came seeking me," said Guenever. "And find me as you see me now."

"Was that for Arthur's sake?" said Lancelot.

And Guenever told him, "It was through my love for you and yours for me that all these ills have come about, and my Lord Arthur is slain or gone from us, and the realm of Logres is no more. Therefore, when Sir Bedivere's letter reached me, I came here secretly, and with those of my maidens who love me best. And in this quiet place I took upon me my vows, to dwell here, a nun, all the days of my life that may be left to me, praying for my soul's-heal, and that God may forgive me my sinning and you yours. Praying also for the souls of my Lord the King and those, the very flowers of knighthood, who died on Camlann Plain."

"The King's death is not sure," said Lancelot, not

seeking to change her resolve, but only to speak some comfort to her.

But she shook her head. "Not in my lifetime will he come back; not in yours . . ." And then she said, "In this world, you and I must meet no more. Therefore I set you free, as never I was strong enough to do before. Get back to your own land, and take a wife and live with her in joy. But let you remember always, love, to pray for me, that God may forgive me my sins and grant me my soul's-heal."

"Nay, sweet madam," said Sir Lancelot, "I have loved you since the day that I was made knight, and I grow too old to be changing my ways. Well you know that for your sake I will wed with no lady, though you give me my freedom a hundred times. Never will I be false to you, but I will keep sweet company with you in another way; for the vows that you have taken upon you, I will take also; and change my knightly harness for a hermit's garb, and pass the rest of my days in prayer and fasting." He smiled with great gentleness, the old twisted smile. "But always my chief prayers shall be for you, that you shall find peace and your soul's-heal."

"Pray for your own," said Guenever. "Pray for your own."

"That will I. But you know well that I was never one gifted with prayer, though that was not for lack of trying. Therefore if my praying will suffice for but one of us, I shall do well enough, thinking that your soul is maybe the lighter for my prayers. I believe that God will not begrudge me that."

And he put out his hand to touch her. But she drew back. "Nay," she said, "never again."

His hand fell to his side, and they looked at each other, the one long moment. And the whitethroat in the medlar tree was singing, singing as though the heart would burst within his breast.

Then Guenever turned and walked away. And Lancelot stood watching her go, until the shadows of the cloister had gathered her into themselves. And then he turned and made for the outer courtyard where his horse was waiting for him, blundering as he went, like a man who has lost his sight.

So Sir Lancelot rode on westward, making for the marshlands close about Avalon, and seeking always for further news of King Arthur. And so he came one evening up from a country of reeds and winding waterways and damp alder woods on to higher ground, and saw before him a wattle-built chapel with a cluster of patched-up bothies around it, all set between two hills, and heard a little bell that rang to Mass.

And Sir Lancelot dismounted and led his horse up the last slope, and hitched its bridle to the low-hanging branch of an ancient apple tree, beside the chapel; and he went in to hear Mass.

It was dim and shadowy within the chapel, after the westering sunlight that had filled his eyes outside, and at first he did not know the aged and withered holy man with scarcely any voice left to him who celebrated the Mass for the great Archbishop Dubricius; but little by little, as though his eyes and his heart cleared together, the recognition came to him, and he knew also that the brown-robed brother who aided him was Sir Bedivere. He was not surprised, but accepted them as right and fitting; and he saw that they knew him and accepted his coming as right and fitting also, the most natural thing in all the world.

And when the Mass was over, they welcomed him and bade him come with them to their living quarters, and there they supped on black rye bread and spring water, and spoke together of the things nearest to their hearts.

"What of the King?" Lancelot asked.

But they could tell him no more than Bedivere had already told in his letter to the Queen. And Lancelot was puzzled. "But this place is Avalon," he said, half in question. "Bedivere, you said – the King said he was for Avalon, to be healed of his wound."

"Also that if I heard of him never more in this life, I was to pray for his soul," said Bedivere in his brown hermit's habit.

Lancelot shook his head. He was too spent and weary to think, but he had looked to find Arthur here, or to be shown his grave.

"But this is Avalon," he said again.

And the old Archbishop saw his bewilderment, and answered him kindly, never knowing that he did so almost in the words that Merlin had spoken to the young Arthur on the day that he received Excalibur. "Avalon of the Apple Trees is not like to other places. It is a threshold place between the world of men and the Land of the Living. Here we are in the Avalon of mortal men. But there is another Avalon. The King is here but he is gone beyond the mist."

Merlin would have understood what he meant; but Merlin was thirty years and more asleep beneath his magic hawthorn tree, and Sir Lancelot was too weary to understand.

But he knew that he had come to the end of his journeyings.

"Will you receive me into your fellowship?" he said at last. "And give shelter and grazing to my horse, for he has served me well."

"That will we, and gladly," said Sir Bedivere.

And the old Archbishop said, "Welcome, my son."

So Sir Lancelot laid by his knightly harness, he who had been the best of all the knights of Christendom, and took upon him the brown habit that the others wore.

When the full month had gone by, and there was no word from Sir Lancelot, the war-host waiting at Dover made ready to depart, as he had bidden them. But Sir Bors himself, and Sir Ector of the Marsh, Sir Blamore and Sir Bleoberis and certain others of Sir Lancelot's kin and closest friends chose to remain in Britain and seek until they found him if he lived, or gained sure word of his fate if he were dead. And so they parted and, singly, they rode Britain from end to end, seeking their lost leader.

And so one day Sir Bors happened on the chapel and its little gathering of huts between two hills, and the ancient apple trees snowy with blossom, for it was spring; and a warhorse grazing quietly below the chapel, among the lesser apple trees that grew there. And he heard a little bell ringing to Mass.

And when he hitched his horse to the lower branch of the tree beside the chapel, and went to answer the call of the bell, there within were three brown-clad brethren; and one of them, so old that only the life

in his brilliant eyes seemed still to bind him to the
world of men, was the Archbishop, and one was
Sir Bedivere, and one was Sir Lancelot of the Lake.
Sir Bors knew that his search was finished. And after
they had shared Mass together, he begged the Archbishop that he might join them.

So Sir Bors also changed his knightly gear for a
rough brown habit, and loosed his horse to graze
beside Lancelot's, and turned him to a life of prayer
and fasting for what remained of his days.

And within half a year, came Sir Blamore and Sir
Bleoberis, and by little and little, certain others of the
old lost brotherhood of the Round Table. And when
in due time the ancient Archbishop died, Sir Lancelot,
whom he had made a priest while he yet lived, stepped
into his place, and celebrated the Mass for the rest as
he had done, and for all who chanced to pass that
way.

So they continued for seven years, living in prayer
and poverty and giving their help and comfort to all
who sought it; and keeping the last light of Logres
alive as they kept the honey-wax candles burning on
the rough altar, while the darkness flowed in over the
rest of the land. For though Constantine, Duke of
Cornwall and a young and distant kinsman of Arthur,
had taken the High Kingship and led his troops to
battle under the dragon banner, he was not Arthur,
and there was little that he could do against the Sea
Wolves, and the Old People from the mountains and
the North.

And the seven years went by; and then one night,
and three times in the same night, Lancelot dreamed
that Guenever lay dying, and that she called to him,

not to come to her while she lived, but to come none the less, with seven of the brethren, and a horse-bier, to fetch her body away to Avalon for burial.

So he arose, and woke the others, and they made a horse-litter of willow saplings, and chose out the two of their warhorses that were oldest and wisest and most gentled with age; and then they set out for Almesbury, the eight of them walking barefoot all the way.

And though from Avalon to Almesbury is but thirty miles, yet the journey took them three days, for they were growing old, and no longer strong to walk long distances as they had used to be. And when they reached Almesbury and came to the nunnery, Guenever had died quietly in the night before their coming.

And when Sir Lancelot was brought to the chamber where she lay, still in her habit, with her hands folded on her breast, those who stood about them saw how he looked long into her face, and did not weep, but gave one great heavy sigh that sounded as though it might have been the going out of his own soul.

Next morning the body of Lady Guenever was laid upon the horse-litter, and with Lancelot and the brethren walking four on either side, they set out to bear her back to Avalon.

And when they reached the little abbey church, they made her a grave before the altar, and wrapped her close in softest silk that the sisters of the nunnery had made ready for her, and Sir Lancelot himself sang her funeral Mass. And they laid her in her quiet grave and strewed the flowers of late summer over her, and made an end.

But from that day, Sir Lancelot began to sicken like an old, tired hound. He scarcely ate or drank, and grew gaunt as a shadow, pining and dwindling away. And within six weeks from the time that he laid the Lady Guenever in her grave, he too was dead.

And while he lay awaiting burial, before the altar, Sir Ector of the Marsh his half-brother, who had for seven years been seeking him, came to Avalon, and saw torches burning in the church, through the windy autumn dusk, and heard the sound of slow and stately chanting. And he dismounted, and hitched his horse to the lowest fruit-laden branch of the ancient apple tree that grew beside the place, and drawn by something, he scarcely knew what, went in through the open door.

Inside he saw brown-clad brethren kneeling in the wind-fretted torchlight, and one who lay before the altar with his big bony hands folded on his breast. And he knelt down just within the door, and waited. And in a while, when the chanting ended, and the brethren rose and turned to see who the newcomer might be, then he knew them in the same instant that they knew him. And the old man who had been Sir Bors came to him gently, holding out his hands.

And Sir Ector looked among them, from Sir Bedivere to Sir Bleoberis and the rest, and asked, "Have you any word of Sir Lancelot? I have sought him these seven years and more."

"Your search is over," said Sir Bors, and led him towards the altar, the others standing back to let him through as though he had some special right. Then he was standing beside the body that lay there, looking down at it. And for three full heart-beats of time even then, he did not know whose it was, for Lancelot had so wasted away over the past weeks that scarce might any man know him for Sir Lancelot of the Lake, fore-most among all the knights of Christendom.

Then as he stood wondering, while the autumn wind swooped round the chapel and the torchlight flared and guttered, he saw that the hands folded on the dead man's breast were a swordsman's hands and a horseman's hands, and the gaunt face with its two sides that did not match with each other was the face of Lancelot his brother.

Sir Ector gave a choking cry and flung aside his sword and shield so that they fell with a clash and clangour upon the rough paved floor. And the great sorrowing words rushed from his heart into his throat and seemed to choke there, and then broke free.

"There, Sir Lancelot, there thou liest, thou that were never matched of earthly knight's hand. And thou were the courtliest knight that ever bore shield. And thou were the truest friend to thy lover that ever bestrode horse. And thou were the truest lover of a sinful man that ever loved woman. And thou were the kindest man that ever struck with sword. And thou were the goodliest person that ever came among press of knights. And thou wast the the meekest man and the gentlest that ever sat in hall among ladies. And thou were the sternest knight to thy mortal foe that ever set spear in rest."

And he knelt, and kissed his brother upon the forehead, and with grief and weariness fell half-swooning beside him.

So Sir Lancelot also was grave-laid, and his great tortured heart found peace at last.

Sir Bedivere and several of the brotherhood remained at the little church and its hermitage all the rest of their days, gathering others to them, so that at last the place became an abbey again; and later still, mighty and beautiful stone buildings arose where the little wattle church and its surrounding bothies had been. And men began to call it Glastonbury.

But Sir Bors and Sir Ector, Sir Bleoberis and Sir Blamore went afar off, into the Holy Land, and there died upon a Good Friday for God's sake.

And save for a valiant glimmer here and there, the darkness flooded in over Britain.

But Sir Lancelot had once said to the King his friend, while they walked at sunset in the narrow orchard below the walls of Camelot, "We shall have made such a blaze that men will remember us on the other side of the dark."

And indeed he had spoken truth, for the stories of Arthur and his knights are told and re-told even to this day.